HUNTED

Chosen by fate. Destined for conflict.

JEDI QUEST

STAR WARS®

BOBA FETT™

HUNTED

ELIZABETH HAND

LUCAS BOOKS

SCHOLASTIC INC.

New York   Toronto   London   Auckland   Sydney
Mexico City   New Delhi   Hong Kong   Buenos Aires

For my son, Tristan
— EH

www.starwars.com
www.scholastic.com

No part of this publication may be reproduced in whole or in part, or stored in a retrieval system, or transmitted in any form or by any means, electronic, mechanical, photocopying, recording, or otherwise, without written permission of the publisher. For information regarding permission, write to Scholastic Inc., Attention: Permissions Department, 557 Broadway, New York, NY 10012.

ISBN 0-439-33930-8

Cover art by Louise Bova

12 11 10 9 8 7 6 5   6 7 8/0

Printed in the U.S.A.
First printing, October 2003

CHAPTER ONE

Some people believe that space is empty. Boba Fett's father, Jango Fett, had been one of those people.

"Space is emptiness," Jango had told his son. "And emptiness is useless, until it is filled with work, or energy, or people, or starships. A good bounty hunter may seem invisible at times. But he knows how to use the space around him. And if he is using that space, it is not empty."

Boba did not think space was empty. Gazing out at the space that surrounded his ship, *Slave I*, he thought that space was full, and brilliant, and beautiful. There were planets everywhere, and stars. He saw distant flares of green, or gold, or red that were nebulas, or galaxies, or even vast starships.

Still, he did agree with his father on one thing. No matter what intergalactic space was, Boba knew he had to make the most of it.

"Approaching destination," a cool, computerized voice from *Slave I*'s controls informed him. "Approaching Tatooine."

Boba leaned forward. He ran his hand across *Slave I*'s piloting console. His fingers touched buttons, switches, and skin-sensitive navigational aids. He smiled.

He was part of the complex space inside this starship. *His* starship, since his father's death. Just days ago, on the planet Aargau, Boba had seized *Slave I* back from Aurra Sing, the notorious bounty hunter who had stolen it from him.

Aargau was the galaxy's banking planet. There, Boba had also regained what remained of his father's fortune — just enough credits to spend on outfitting *Slave I* for this journey.

"Estimated time of landing, 01200 mesarcs," the computer said. "Breaching Tatooine airspace."

Tatooine.

Boba Fett stared out at the planet before him. It was a vast bone-colored sphere, streaked here and there with darker brown and white. In the distance, Tatooine's twin suns blazed dull orange. They were like demonic eyes staring back at Boba.

No, space was not empty.

He leaned forward and punched a command into the control console. With a dull roar, *Slave I* pierced the desert planet's atmosphere. The ship began to hurtle toward Tatooine's surface. The twin suns grew smaller, less bright. But they remained ominous. Boba gazed out at the desert world, grimacing.

This sure isn't a place where you'd want to spend much time, he thought.

Sandstorms, oceans of sand dunes, drought-stricken canyons, moisture farms, and unrelenting heat. From what Boba had heard, Tatooine filled its own space with some pretty awful stuff.

So remind me why I'm going here?

Boba smiled grimly. He knew the answer to that question.

His father, Jango, had been killed by a Jedi Knight named Mace Windu. But as one of the galaxy's greatest bounty hunters (*the* greatest, in Boba's opinion), Jango had lived every day knowing that he might die.

And he had loved his son. To prepare Boba in case the worst ever happened, Jango had left him a book. In this book were screens of information, advice, and encouragement. All were written in his father's own words. Sometimes the book showed his father's own image, too.

"Hold onto this book," Jango Fett's face and voice told him when Boba looked inside the book. "Keep it close to you. Open it when you need it. It will guide you when you need guidance. It is not a story but a Way. Follow this Way and someday you will be a great bounty hunter, Boba."

That was what Boba wanted more than anything. To be a great bounty hunter, like his father had been. To know that his father would have been proud of him.

Sometimes, late at night when he was alone and scrolling through the book, Boba pretended that his father was still alive, somewhere.

But he could never pretend that for very long.

Now the book was in his pocket. Boba did not need to look at it. He knew the advice it held for him regarding Tatooine.

"For knowledge you must find Jabba," the book said. "He will not give it; you must take it."

Jabba the Hutt! One of the galaxy's most notorious gangsters and crime lords! And Tatooine's most famous, if disgusting, resident.

Jabba was why Boba was about to make landfall on this forsaken, desolate planet.

Boba had already found Tyranus. That was how Boba had ended up on Aargau. Tyranus was the agent who had selected Jango Fett to be the source for the Republic's clone army.

But Tyranus was also Count Dooku, who was leading the Republic's enemies, the Separatists.

And only Boba had the knowledge that these two people were the same.

Knowledge is power, his father had always told him. But even the power of knowledge could be limited.

For knowledge you must find Jabba. He will not give it; you must take it.

Boba had escaped from Aurra Sing and Aargau, but he needed more credits to survive. He needed more power. He needed more knowledge. He took a deep breath, then reached for the console and entered the coordinates for Mos Espa, Tatooine's bustling spaceport.

"Prepare for landing," he said to his ship, and to himself.

Boba hated to admit it, but he needed Jabba the Hutt.

CHAPTER TWO

"Planets are like people," Boba's father always used to say. "They all have individual personalities."

At the time, this hadn't made sense to Boba.

Since then, Boba had learned that it was true.

Kamino, his home world, was gray and grim and cloud-covered, plagued by rains that could last for months on end. The native Kaminoans were like their planet. They were cool and seemingly unchanging, well-mannered but obsessed with control. They were the ideal supervisors for the creation of the clone army.

Aargau, run by the InterGalactic Banking Clan, was strictly ordered on its surface. But underneath that orderly surface was the chaos of the Undercity. In the Undercity, *anything* could happen.

And Tatooine?

As *Slave I* banked, Boba stared at the spaceport below him. It was a jumble of domes, pleasure spires, and gambling minarets. He saw long, low warehouses, and the rusted spines of outdated space-traffic control towers. He saw racing arenas, coliseums, and junkshops. Biggest of all was the enormous Arena Citadel. That was where the Pod-racers began their competition, before hurtling off into the desert.

Everything was coated with a thick layer of dust. Mos Espa's ragtag buildings looked as though they had crawled in from the desert like giant sand-worms, and then collapsed, too exhausted to go on. Beyond the borders of the spaceport stretched the vast expanse of the Dune Sea, wastelands of sand and dust and wind-carved rocks.

If Tatooine has a personality, Boba thought with bleak amusement, *it's a mixed-up one.*

Slave I cruised slowly above the network of docking bays. From here they looked like craters, bristling with surveillance and repair equipment. Droids scurried around them like ants. Boba stared down, trying to determine which docking bay would be safest. He had barely enough credits left to pay for docking, and none for refueling. He'd have no more credits at all until he met with Jabba the Hutt.

What would my father do? he thought.

And suddenly he knew.

He put on his father's Mandalorian helmet,

which, he noticed proudly, fit better than it had just a few months ago. He felt a slight warmth as the helmet's eye sensors scanned his retinas, and then the reassuring hum as the interactive system recognized him.

He searched *Slave I*'s memory banks for the location of the docking facility last used by Jango Fett.

The nav computer informed him that the docks belonged to Mentis Qinx.

Boba punched in the coordinates. He leaned back in the control seat. Smooth as flowing water, the ship banked. It began its descent into a warren of dilapidated towers surrounding a large and very battered docking bay.

Boba smiled. He adjusted the Mandalorian helmet. He checked to make sure his book was in his pocket. Minutes later, *Slave I* landed safely at Mos Espa.

He had made it. But that was only the beginning.

He had to find Jabba.

Boba decided to wear the helmet, at least at first. That way no one would know how young he was. He was dressed in standard-issue Mandalorian uniform — gray-blue tunic and trousers, darker shirt, high black boots. With the helmet covering his face, he might be anyone of small stature. He might be a Mrlssi physicist, or a Bimm merchant, or a Sullustan pilot.

Nobody had to know he was just a kid.

He cleared his throat, then clambered out of Slave I and into the docking bay.

The air of Tatooine struck him like a fist. Hot, dry air, so saturated with grit and dust that he could taste it on his tongue, despite the protective helmet. A few meters away, small service droids scurried and rolled beneath another ship. There were fuel lines and repair equipment scattered everywhere. Boba looked around for someone in charge, standing as straight as he could to project confidence.

"Sir!" a smooth voice greeted him, recognizing the ship. "Jango Fett, is it?"

A gleaming figure was approaching him — a silver-plated 3D-4X administrative droid. Its blunt, tube-shaped head whirled as it looked from Boba to Slave I.

"Fett, that's right," Boba said. He felt a small surge of relief. A droid would be easier to fool than a human or an alien. "I need to leave my ship here for a while."

"Very good, very good," said the droid. It halted. Boba could hear a garbled stream of syllables coming through its communications transmitter. After a moment it turned back to him. "Master Qinx wishes you to be reminded that there is a small matter of an outstanding debit on your account."

Boba swallowed. Inside the helmet his face felt as though it were melting. He took a deep breath, squared his shoulders and said, "I am aware of that. Here —"

Boba held out a credit chip, all that remained of his father's fortune. The droid scanned it, then rotated its head.

"That is not enough."

"I'm aware of that, too," Boba said quickly. He was glad the droid couldn't see his face. "Please inform your master that I have a private audience with Jabba the Hutt regarding some old business of my own. Once I've met with Jabba, I'll make payment in full."

"Master Quinx specifically stated that —"

Boba shook his head. "I am certain that your master would not want to make me late for my meeting with Jabba," he said in the warning tone he'd heard his father use so many times. "Of course, I can inform Jabba that there will be a delay. . . ."

Boba turned and took a step back toward his ship. His breath came too fast in his throat. What if the droid knew he was bluffing?

Behind him he could hear the whine of the 3D-4X's communicator.

"Very well," the droid said. Its smooth voice sounded slightly anxious. "Of course, we do not want to delay your meeting with Jabba the Hutt. Will there be anything you need upon your return?"

Safe behind his helmet, Boba grinned. *Why not?*

"Yes," he said. "Please provide a full overhaul and restocking of my ship. And refuel it."

"Very well, sir." The droid began to stride purposefully toward the service droids. "You, there! Leave that and get over here immediately!"

Boba watched as the droids began to surround *Slave I,* beeping and whirring. Then he turned and headed for the ramp that led down to the streets.

Maybe this will be easier than I thought! He smoothed the front of his tunic and walked outside, head held high. *Jabba, here I come!*

In less than a minute, he was hopelessly lost.

CHAPTER THREE

From the air, Mos Espa had looked confusing, but not chaotic. Boba had recognized streets and alleys, even major roads leading into the desert. It was all complicated, but he assumed there was a pattern. And if there was a pattern, he would figure out how to use it.

But as soon as he stepped from the overhang of the docking bay, Boba realized there was no pattern here. There was no logic, except the logic of buying and selling and stealing.

For just a moment, Boba forgot about appearing to be in control.

"Wow," he breathed, amazed.

From the air, Mos Espa — all of Tatootine — had seemed to be one color. The color of sand, of dust, of raw rock.

But now that he stood in the middle of it all, Boba saw that was not true. His father had told him once about seeing the world in a grain of sand. That was what Boba felt like he was seeing now.

Around him was a swirl of deep gold, pale buff, almost white. Ancient buildings made of cracked rock and brick; roads of broken stones and alleys of packed dirt. There were water harvesters and rusted tankers, and cracked useless water vaporators.

And there were life-forms everywhere. They hurried past him, shrouded against the relentless wind and dust. He saw groups of tiny Jawas in stained, dirt-colored robes and hoods. Their yellow eyes glowed balefully as they moved on. Some of them rode tall, placid rontos that swung their horned heads to stare calmly at Boba.

There were jabbering merchants, selling water and smuggled goods. There were Feeorin pirates, their faces jowled with indigo tentacles, and beautifully dressed women, heavily jeweled and masked as they made their way to Hutt casinos.

"Magravian spice, m'lord?" a voice hissed at Boba's helmet. "It will make your reflexes sharp as chrsyalide claws!"

Boba shook his head as a snouted Rodian thrust a filthy hand toward him.

"No thanks," Boba said. He took a few quick steps into the street.

"GEGGAOURRAAAY!" a voice shouted.

Boba looked up and saw a huge form bearing down on him. It was a bantha, its large, sloped body swaying back and forth. On its back stood an armed Tusken Raider. Boba stared at it, marvelling: He knew it was rare to see one so far from its desert home.

The Raider yelled threateningly at Boba. Boba couldn't understand what it was saying, but he knew what it meant.

Move!

Boba lunged out of the way. He could feel the bantha's stiff fringe of hair brushing against him as it lumbered past. He heard the *whoosh* of the Raider's staff slicing through the air just above him.

That was close — way too close, Boba thought.

He hurried on. Ahead of him stood a bustling, run-down building: a cantina. Droids and aliens, recent immigrants and Tatooine natives all milled in front of it, or made their way in and out. Suspicious-looking men in dusty robes hawked caged beasts — chittering neeks from Ambria and crablike suuri, phosphorescent boeys in glass globes.

"Young warrior!" a smuggler called in a low voice as Boba passed. "I have blasters, the very finest, very cheap, very fine."

Boba ignored him. Only as he approached the cantina's doors did he slow down.

From inside came the sounds of drunken singing, muffled shouts, the clack of mung-tee balls.

And, best of all, the smell of food.

Boba paused. His mouth was watering. He knew he had no credits left, but maybe he might be able to swipe an unfinished platter of food. Grown-ups were notorious for not cleaning their plates. He looked around, made sure his helmet was on securely, and pushed the door open.

Inside the noise was deafening. So was the hulking Noghri security guard who glared down at Boba.

"Display all your weapons!" he shouted. "This isn't like those cantinas in Mos Eisley — we'll have no firefights here."

Boba raised his empty hands. The Noghri roughly patted him down. Boba held his breath. He was worried that the guard might raise his helmet and see that he was not a warrior of small stature, but a kid.

Luckily, the Noghri had no time for that. Behind Boba a group of rowdy Wookiees appeared.

"Go on, then!" the guard yelled at Boba, gesturing inside. "Next!"

Boba strode through a passage and into the

main room. A long, neon purple bar occupied its center, with tables scattered elsewhere. Piped-in music played, adding to the tumult. There were aliens and humans everywhere, heads bent close together as they plotted and planned, or simply ate and drank. Service droids bustled back and forth, clearing dishes and refilling drinks.

Boba looked around.

"There!" he murmured. Near the back of the room he spied an abandoned table. It still had plates on it. Boba glanced around to make sure no one took note of him. He casually sauntered over to the table.

"Yes!" he whispered to himself. "Jackpot!"

Someone had left an entire roba plate untouched. Beside it steamed a heaping mound of yan legumes. Boba reached out, grabbed the roba and drew it to his mouth.

Still warm! He took a bite, chewed, and swallowed; then reached for the yan.

"Hey!"

Boba gulped. He turned to see a tall woman in a Myrkr pilot's uniform. She scowled at him, her hand resting lightly on the blaster at her hip.

"Uh, sorry," stammered Boba. "I thought this was my table."

Another pilot appeared behind the first. Boba

started to back away, when a crushingly huge hand descended onto his shoulder.

"Mandalorian scum!" said a deep voice. "You dare to breathe the same air as I do?"

Boba twisted. He looked up to see a figure easily three meters tall. From helmeted head to booted feet, he was clad in a shining carapace of armor. He carried a blaster as long as his arm; knives and more blasters hung around his waist.

But worst of all was what he bore on his chest: the livid image of a Mandalorian skull.

"Is there a problem, Durge?" one of the pilots said.

Durge.

Boba stared at him. His hands and neck suddenly went cold. In front of him stood an imposing figure. Inside his helmet, his eyes glowed a malevolent red.

"When I see a Mandalorian," Durge said, raising his arm, "there is always a problem. Especially one that Count Dooku has asked me to hunt down."

CHAPTER FOUR

Boba's heart hammered his chest. But he stood his ground and stared at the figure before him.

Durge! His father had warned Boba about him. A two-thousand-year-old bounty hunter, Durge hated the Mandalorians more than anything else in the galaxy. A hundred years before Boba was born, Durge had attempted to capture the Mandalorians' leader. Instead, he himself was captured and tortured.

But Durge escaped. He went into hibernation to recover from his wounds. When he emerged fully healed, he vowed revenge upon all Mandalorians.

Yet it was too late for revenge. By then, there were few Mandalorians left in the galaxy. They had been exterminated in the course of countless battles, some with the Jedi.

Still, part of Jango Fett remained alive in the clone army generated from his DNA. Durge had vowed to eliminate all of Jango's clones . . . and do Count Dooku's bidding.

What would he do if he knew that Jango's true son stood before him?

I'm not gonna wait to find out, thought Boba grimly.

He took a deep breath. Just as Durge's fist came smashing down toward him, Boba dove between the bounty hunter's legs.

Good thing he's so tall! Boba hit the floor running.

"Get him!"

Boba raced for the door. Service droids bleeped and scurried away. Near the door, three Wookiees backed against the wall, giving deep bellows of excitement.

BLAAAAAMM!

A burst of blaster fire ricocheted overhead. Boba could hear shouts and a blast of answering fire.

"Hey, you!" shouted the Noghri guard as the young bounty hunter whizzed by. The guard snatched at him, but Boba was too fast. In seconds he was outside again.

"Glad I'm outta there!" he gasped.

He kept running, until the cantina was out of sight behind him. There were still throngs of people everywhere, but no one seemed to notice him at all.

Probably used to folks being chased, thought Boba. He turned and continued running down a side street.

He was starting to get tired. *I better rest soon, before I —*

With a grunt, Boba tripped on a pile of rubble. Crying out, he fell forward onto a cracked sidewalk. Instinctively his hands reached out to break his fall.

But it wasn't enough to keep him from crashing onto the hard, dusty ground.

"*Oooof —*"

He went down, headfirst, hard enough that the breath was knocked out of him. Too late he remembered his helmet.

"No!"

Helplessly, Boba felt the helmet bounce from his head. He grabbed at it. For just an instant, he felt its smooth metal surface. Then it slid from his grasp.

It was gone.

Around him was a sea of legs and feet — booted feet, hooved feet, clawed feet.

Where was his helmet?

Frantically, Boba scrambled forward on his hands and knees. He ignored the curses and jeers of those who had to step around him. A booted foot kicked at him. Someone else laughed. Boba gritted his teeth and kept going.

There!

He could just see it, only an arm's length away. There was the familiar smooth sweep of black that hid his face when the helmet was where it belonged.

Boba stumbled to his feet, his hand stretched out to grab the helmet.

And just as he did, someone else snatched it from him!

"Looking for something?"

Boba straightened, furious. "That's mine! Give it to me!"

"Yours?" The voice snorted in disbelief. "I don't think so."

Boba looked up. In front of him stood a girl. She was maybe a year younger than he was. She was smaller than Boba, and much dirtier. Her face was streaked with dust and soot. So was her hair. It looked brown, but Boba suspected it might be dark blond beneath the layer of grime. She was skinny, almost starved-looking, and wore tattered cast-off clothes — an Ugnaught mechanic's smock, much too big and belted around the waist with a piece of filthy rope. Her eyes were blue and piercing.

She might have been younger than he was, but she looked just as determined.

"Where would *you* get a Mandalorian battle helmet?" she demanded. She held it up and stared at it thoughtfully. "This is worth a *lot*," she continued. She gave Boba a look that was both suspicious and admiring. "Where'd you steal it?"

"I didn't!" He lunged, grabbing for it, but she was too fast. Before he could say another word, she was already on the far side of the road, running with the helmet under her arm.

Boba stared after her, stunned.

"No one takes what's mine!" he shouted, and raced in pursuit.

CHAPTER FIVE

The winding road was even more crowded than the one he'd left. But this time, Boba's size helped him. He could wriggle in and out of the throng as quickly as a Ralltiirieel. He could easily keep the girl in view, since she wasn't bigger than he was. He found that he was enjoying the chase.

He followed her, panting, past dark doorways where smugglers lurked, down narrow alleys crowded with pack animals like hairy tybis and immense banthas. He raced through an open marketplace taken up by a huge starship surrounded by twittering Jawas. They were already gutting it to sell on the black market. The girl ran on tirelessly, her bare feet slapping the ground.

"Stop!" Boba yelled.

When he saw the looks the Jawas gave him, he realized yelling was a mistake. After that he ran in silence, saving his energy for the chase.

On and on she ran. Boba had to duck under low

awnings, jump over heaps of rubbish and the steaming remains of a beggar's tiny campfire. But after a few more minutes he began to gain on her. The girl thief was small and fast, and she knew her way around Mos Espa.

Boba was stronger.

And the Mandalorian helmet was heavy and hard for her to carry. He could tell from the way she clutched it to her side. Once she almost dropped it, and Boba thought he'd get it back at last. His hand stretched out, he could feel the rough cloth of her dirty smock and the smooth curve of his helmet . . .

With a cry she yanked the helmet closer, hugging it to her thin chest. She made a sharp turn and ran into a building, Boba at her heels.

He didn't pause to look up and see where he was going. If he had, he might have hesitated. The building was a mere shell. Spindly pieces of wood leaned against each other to form a doorway. A ragged piece of cloth dangled in front of it like a discarded shroud.

But Boba didn't bother to stop. He raced after her. Seconds later he was plunged into darkness.

He halted, struggling for breath. He cocked his head, listening. He could hear someone else panting.

The girl.

"I know you're there," he said. Suddenly, he was so angry he didn't stop to think of what his father would do in a place like this — which would *not* have been what Boba did next.

Without looking around, he stuck his hand in front of him. Then he stepped forward.

Something soft brushed his leg. He moved away, thinking it was a piece of the dirty cloth in the doorway.

It wasn't. Before he could blink, hands covered his eyes. Other hands grabbed him by the ankles, yanking him down.

"Hey —!"

"Not a word, stranger."

He tensed, lifting his hand to strike out. Then he felt something cold against his throat.

A knife.

"If you move, you're dead," someone said in a low voice.

Boba took a deep breath, forcing his body to go limp. Hands patted him down, slid into his pocket, and closed around his book.

"Here's something!"

Without thinking Boba started to yank it back. The icy blade pressed harder against his throat. Boba used every ounce of his will to remain motionless.

"What is it?" someone whispered.

"A book."

The first someone made a scornful noise. "A book? Who needs a *book*? Get rid of it!"

"Give it to me!" Boba recognized the voice of the girl thief. "If you'd ever *read* a book, Murzz, you might have been able to grow a brain between your ears."

He heard scuffling, then a muffled cry; then the girl's voice again.

"Wow. Look at this!" This time she didn't sound suspicious — just admiring. "Let's see what else he's got!"

More small hands checked his pockets, his cuffs, even the inside of his boots. They found nothing.

I could save you all a lot of trouble, thought Boba fiercely, *if you'd let me go!*

He stared at the blackness that surrounded him. He blinked. His eyes were starting to grow accustomed to the dark. He could just make out a shadowy form kneeling at his side — the person who held the blade to his throat. There were two — no, three — other, smaller figures moving around him.

None of them seemed to be the girl. He squinted, but he still couldn't see her.

But he could hear her.

"Keep looking!" she commanded from the shadows. "Whoever this boy is, he's got some interesting cargo. *Very* interesting."

Small fingers danced across Boba's cheeks, tapping his ears and then his mouth.

They're looking for jewels, Boba thought. *And gold teeth.*

He lay motionless, waiting until one of the fingers thrust into his mouth. Then he bit down.

Hard.

"Owwwww!"

Figures scampered away from him into the cavernous room. Boba grabbed the hand at his throat. He twisted it until he heard a groan, followed by the soft clatter of metal hitting the ground. Boba struck out blindly. He felt his hand smack into a small form that went sprawling. Boba scrambled to his feet, grabbing the person who'd fallen beside him.

"Ygabba, help!"

"Be quiet!" said Boba. He yanked the figure up again. Through the darkness he glimpsed a small, thin face, matchstick arms, and a wild frizz of black hair like smoke.

Just a kid. He was a lot smaller and younger than Boba, too.

Boba felt a stab of pity. But then he remembered the cold touch of the blade at his throat. He glanced down and saw a glint of silver near his foot. Still keeping a tight hold on the boy, Boba stooped and grabbed the blade. He glared into the shadows.

"Give me back my helmet," he shouted. "Otherwise —"

"Otherwise what?"

It was the girl. By now he could see well enough to recognize her as she stepped toward him. She held up a small plasteel torch and switched it on. Bright white light flooded the room. Boba shaded his face. At his side the small boy writhed and tried to get free.

"You won't hurt him," the girl went on. She stared at Boba with eyes brilliant and piercing as the torchlight. "You're not like us."

You're not like us. She made it sound like a dare.

Boba glared back at her and said, "No, I'm not. I'm not a thief, for one."

"Oh, no?" The girl gave him a cold smile. She held up the Mandalorian helmet — *his* helmet — and the book. *His* book. "Then how'd you get this? And this?"

Boba stared back at her just as coldly. "Those are mine."

At his side the small boy began to whimper.

Boba looked down at him. "Be quiet," he whispered.

Boba looked at the blade in his own hand, and then at the girl. He saw a flicker of unease cross her thin face.

Unease? Or could it be fear?

Fear is your friend, if it is your enemy's fear, his father used to say.

But the girl did not seem afraid of Boba. She continued to stare at him defiantly. He saw her gaze dart to the boy he held captive.

She's not afraid of me, Boba thought. *She's afraid for him.*

"Give my things back to me and I'll let him go," Boba said. "See?" He held up the blade, then slid it into his belt. "All I want is what's mine."

An edge of desperation crept into his voice. Not because he was afraid — though he was, of course. Only a fool is never afraid.

I can't lose those. He felt the pit of his stomach grow cold, as though someone held a knife there. *That's all I have of him.*

"Yours?" The girl gave a bitter laugh. "I don't believe it. But —"

She stepped toward him. Behind her, Boba could glimpse the other children standing watchfully.

"You must be very clever, or very lucky, to have

gotten your hands on a Mandalorian battle helmet," she went on. "We are always looking for clever recruits. And lucky ones."

Boba shook his head. "I'm not interested. I work alone."

A hard smile crept slowly across the girl's thin face. "Then you won't last very long on Tatooine," she said. "And you'll need all the luck you can get."

Slowly she raised her arm, her hand curled into a fist. The other children did the same. Boba stared at them. Like poisonous flowers blooming, the children's fists unclenched. They held them up, palm out, so that Boba could see.

In the center of every palm was a single eye. And every one of them was fixed on Boba Fett.

CHAPTER SIX

"What — what are those?" Boba stammered.

"The Master's eyes," the girl called Ygabba replied calmly.

"The Master?"

Without another word the girl turned and walked into the darkness. Boba stared after her, confused and unnerved. At his side the small boy gave a pitiful wail. Boba looked down, ashamed — he'd almost forgotten him.

"Ygabba!" the boy cried. The girl kept going without a backward glance. "Ygabba, *please,* wait!"

Boba felt guilty. He steeled himself at the thought of those lidless eyes. His hold on the boy's wrist loosened, just a fraction.

But that was enough. With a shrill laugh the boy yanked his hand free. He slipped from Boba's grasp and ran gleefully after the others. Boba groaned and followed.

It took only minutes for him to catch up. The dim

room narrowed to a single tunneling passage. Its walls were made of some flimsy transparent material. Sand had seeped through gashes in the sides. He could see the others a short distance ahead of him. They were walking with no real urgency. He could hear laughter, and snatches of conversation.

". . . will the Master be happy now?"

"I don't care, as long as he feeds us!"

"*Shhh,* all of you!"

Ahead of him Boba saw the tunnel widen into a circular opening. It glowed a dull orange. As the others ran through, they looked like black shadow puppets against a fire. Last of all came Boba. He peered around in search of the girl thief.

"Welcome, stranger," her voice greeted him.

He looked up. There she was, perched on a high metal shelf. She lifted her hand and he could see the extra eye watching him. Her bare legs swung back and forth. His helmet was in her lap.

"Don't worry," she said. "They can't hurt you. The eyes, I mean."

Boba turned, looking around in amazement.

He was inside the cabin of a starship. Not just any starship, either, but a Theed Cruiser — he recognized it from blueprints he'd studied in his father's quarters back on Kamino.

"How — how did this get here?" he asked.

"Same way a Mandalorian helmet got into your hands," said the girl, and laughed. "Someone stole it."

She picked up his helmet. For a long moment she looked at it. Then she turned and stuffed it into some kind of storage compartment. She punched in a security code. The compartment door slid shut. She stood, looking down at Boba's anguished face.

"Don't worry," she said. She stepped to the edge of the shelf, swung herself down, and walked over to Boba. "It's safer there," she added in a low voice. "Trust me."

"Trust you?" Boba started to shout. "You —"

The girl motioned at him to be quiet. He glimpsed the eye in her hand, its pupil black as the darkest ink. She raised her eyebrows, silently indicating the vast room around them.

Boba's mouth clamped shut. He turned and looked around.

It wasn't an entire cruiser, he saw now. Just the cabin. Huge ragged gashes showed where the wings and the power generators had been removed. What remained was a long, high chamber. Bare wires and scorched coils of metal hung from the ceiling. There were holes in the floor. The dull orange light came from lumen globes suspended overhead like immense insect eggs. Bits of shattered circuitry were everywhere, and broken tiles, and remnants of what looked like weaponry — electromagnetic pulse guns, proton torpedo casings, phasers.

And, everywhere, there were children. Dozens of them. They perched on the metal shelves that circled the chamber, staring down at him with hungry, feral eyes. He had never seen humans or aliens so thin, not even the Kaminoans. They were of as many different races and colors as the galaxy could hold — children from Alderaan, Kalarba, Tatooine; green-eyed Kuats, young Dathomir witches, otterlike Selonians.

The only thing they had in common, as far as Boba could see, was that they all looked starved. They all looked afraid. And every one of them had an extra eye.

CHAPTER SEVEN

"Who — who are you?" Boba turned to the thief. "What is this place?"

"I'm Ygabba." The girl smoothed the front of her filthy tunic. She looked uneasy. "And this is the stronghold of the Master's army."

"Army?" Boba looked at the emaciated figures staring down at him. "My father always said an army travels on its stomach. Doesn't look like this one's going anywhere."

Shocked murmurs came from the watching figures. Ygabba shook her head. "I wouldn't talk like that if I were you," she said in a low voice. "The Master wouldn't be too happy."

"Master? What Master?" Boba stared at her. "I don't see anyone in charge here."

The children whispered. Ygabba gave an anxious glance over her shoulder. "I mean it," she said. "You better not —"

Her eyes suddenly widened.

"Master!" she gasped. She raised her hands before her face, then dropped to the floor, cowering. "Master Libkath . . ."

Boba whirled to see what she stared at. The air flickered and brightened as though shining sand was being poured into an invisible bottle. Slowly, slowly, an alien form appeared in the middle of the chamber. He was tall and thin, clad in deep-blue shimmering robes. He looked even taller because of the hat he wore, a gleaming black mitre like a crown. His hands were gnarled and sickly white, as was his face. His eyes were huge and round. They glowed the same dull orange as the chamber's lumen globes. With terrible slow care he raised his head and stared intently into the room. When he spoke, his voice was disturbingly gentle. It had a quiet hiss like a boiling kettle.

"Who am I?" he asked.

There was a hushed intake of breath in the chamber. The children raised their hands. In every one a cold eye gleamed.

"You are our Master, Libkath," the children said as one.

The tall figure nodded. "That is so. Who cares for you, children?"

"You do, Master."

"Who gives you refuge?" he asked.

"You do, Master," repeated the children.

The eyes stared at the figure. He stared back. After a moment he nodded again.

"That is so." A half-smile crawled across his reptilian face. "And what do I ask in return?"

"Obedience, Master."

"Very good." The figure lifted its hands, turning. Boba felt his stomach clench as those round, glowing eyes fixed on him.

"There will be many people at the Podraces tonight," the figure said. "That means there will be many vessels parked outside the Arena Citadel. Many guards, but also many unwary soldiers who will have had too much to drink. A shipment of smuggled weapons will be outside the northwest gate. You are to bring them here."

The children whispered, "Yes, Master."

The figure stared straight at Boba. "What does failure mean?" he hissed.

Boba opened his mouth but said nothing.

"Failure means destruction," said Master Libkath. "Do not fail."

And with a blinding flash, the figure disappeared.

CHAPTER EIGHT

Boba blinked. It took him a minute to register exactly what he had seen.

Not an actual person at all, but a holo. A virtual sending.

He had never been in any real danger. Master Libkath, whoever he was, had not really been there. He had not seen Boba at all, but Boba had recognized him as a Neimoidian. He'd met Neimoidians before, on Geonosis.

Still, Libkath had been frightening, at least for the others. Even Boba hadn't been able to look at those weird eyes without getting a queasy feeling. For a moment he couldn't speak. The chamber around him, too, was silent. Then, all at once, the children began babbling and talking.

"No time!" shouted Ygabba. She spun on her heel and headed for a jagged opening that had once housed a power generator. "You heard the Master — we have work to do!"

"But I'm hungry," someone whined.

"Me, too," yelled someone else.

"And me!" piped in another.

Ygabba stopped. Her face looked tired and worn, and much older. "I know," she said. "I'm hungry, too. There will be food vendors outside the arena."

"But we have nothing to trade," said a small Tatooine boy.

A grin spread across Ygabba's face. "That never stopped us before!" she said. The others laughed.

Boba walked up beside her.

"So you're *all* thieves," he said accusingly. He grabbed her arm. "Well, I'm not. I want my things. Give them to me and I'll go."

Ygabba looked him up and down.

"What do you know about us?" she said at last. "You'd steal, too, if you were starving. Many of us have been separated from our families. Others watched as their parents were killed by thugs."

Her brilliant blue eyes stared at him. Boba stared back.

"I saw my father killed, too," he said quietly. "I know what it's like to be alone. I know what it's like not to trust." He shook his head. "But I've never stolen anything in my life. And I won't start now."

The girl looked at him. Her expression softened.

"Your father," she said. "That helmet — it was his?"

Boba nodded.

"And the book?"

"Yes," said Boba.

Ygabba stood there, thinking. Finally she reached into her pocket.

"Here," she said. She handed him his book. "I'm sorry we took it."

Boba slid it into his packet. "What about my helmet?"

"No." She looked behind them, to where the other children milled around. They were waiting for her to lead them out. "What I told you was true. It's safer here. There are many, many thieves in Mos Espa. Bigger ones than us. Scarier ones. I'll give you your helmet back later. I promise."

"That's not good enough. I need it," said Boba. It was not a plea, but a command. "Now."

The girl stared at him for a long time. Finally she nodded.

"All right," she said. She turned and climbed back onto the shelf and opened the storage compartment. A minute later she returned with the helmet.

"Here," she said.

She held it out to Boba. He grasped it, but her hands did not let go.

"You owe me for this," she said, and drew her hands back.

"Owe you?" said Boba hotly. He clutched the helmet to his chest. "For stealing my helmet?"

"No. For teaching you to be more careful with it."

The girl walked away, gesturing for some of the other children to come with her to find food. Boba watched her, then followed, the helmet still in his hands.

"Maybe you're right," he said grudgingly. "But I'm still not going to become a thief."

Ygabba shrugged. "Suit yourself."

She pushed at a piece of scrap metal that served as a door, and stepped out into an alley choked with garbage. "Sooner or later, people like us end up here with Libkath. There's no place else to go."

Boba followed her outside. "Who is Libkath?" he asked.

"An exiled Neimoidian," said the girl. "At least, I think he's an exile. I'm not sure. The other kids, they don't even wonder who he really is. But I do. All the time. He gives us shelter and food. Not much, but better than nothing. He protects us from the Hutt gangsters. In return we do what he asks."

"Do you ever actually see him?" said Boba. "I mean, the real him, and not just a holo."

"Yes." Ygabba shuddered. "Believe me — the holo is better."

Boba thought of those evil glowing eyes boring into him. "I'll take your word for it. What about those?"

He pointed to her hand. Ygabba lifted it, opening her palm so that he could see the lidless eye in its center. "It's a tracer orb," she explained. "Advanced nanotechnology and organic matter. When the Master takes us, he has a med droid implant these in our hands."

"Does he watch everything you do with them?"

"No. They're monitors, that's all. If we leave the planet, they're programmed to release a toxin into our bloodstream."

"That's awful!"

"I know. That's why we listen to him. That's why we do what he asks. We have no choice."

Boba listened thoughtfully. "Do you ever really see him?" he asked. "Or does he only communicate like that?"

"Oh, we see him, all right. Him and his battle droids," said Ygabba grimly. "Whenever we perform a mission. He has us do his dirty work — stealing weapons, or crystal fuel, or water. Sometimes he has us hide things for him. Then he comes back here and collects the goods. He takes them away and sells them."

Boba nodded. "I get it," he said. "He's smuggling weapons!"

Ygabba shrugged. "I guess so. All I know is that he takes whatever we steal for him. He gets the fortune, and we get scraps. If we're lucky."

"Does he work alone?"

"No," said Ygabba. "He has soldiers. Mercenaries. And droids."

She began to walk down the alley. She picked her way carefully among dead weeds and heaps of burned-out circuitry. Boba stayed at her side. He didn't put the helmet on yet. He had a feeling that he might attract more attention if he did.

A Mandalorian warrior, followed by a bunch of ragged children?

The thought made him smile a little. It also made him sad.

If I was a real warrior, I would free them, he thought. *I'd bring them back to their families and make sure the Master paid for this!*

Behind him trailed the children. They pushed at one another, laughing and talking quietly.

Now and then one of them would stop and poke at a heap of rubbish. Once Boba looked back. He saw a boy pull something long and squirming from the ground and pop it into his mouth.

After that, Boba kept his eyes straight ahead.

"Can I ask what you're doing here on Tatooine?" Ygabba asked after they had been walking for a while.

Boba hesitated. "I'm here to find Jabba the Hutt," he said at last.

"Jabba?" Ygabba's blue eyes widened. "You've got a long way to go, then. His palace is at the edge of the Western Dune Sea. That's hundreds of klics from here."

Boba felt a pang of dismay. "Then I'll just have to find a way across the Dune Sea," he said.

"Wait." Ygabba stopped. She put a hand on his arm. "Let me think."

Her brow furrowed. After a second she nodded excitedly. "Yes! I bet I'm right!"

"What?" asked Boba. "Tell me!"

She began walking faster. "There are night Podraces this evening — they're being sponsored by Jabba," she said. "And this shipment of weapons that we're supposed to go after — it's probably for Jabba, too. I'll bet you dinner at KiLargo's Cantina that Jabba will be at the arena."

She snapped her fingers, laughing.

Boba looked at her doubtfully. "Are you sure? How do you know all this stuff?"

"It's my job to know. You'd be surprised what people will say in front of someone our age."

Boba nodded. He thought of how stupid grown-ups could be, and how oblivious they were of what kids really knew.

Ahead of them the alley branched into a wide street. On the far side of the street loomed an immense structure.

The Arena Citadel. It was big enough to be a mountain, though Boba had never seen a mountain so alive. Throngs of beings were everywhere, along with carts and speeders and swoopbikes, braying banthas and armed guards, who shouted at people to keep moving.

"The main gate's there," said Ygabba. " And the northwest gate is that way."

She pointed to the far side of the arena. "But if you want to find Jabba the Hutt, your best bet would be around back, at the southeast gate. That's where the aristos go."

Boba frowned. "Aristos?"

"You know — rich people. The Hutts have their own private entrance. Their own private box. Of course, I have no idea how you'll get in," she added loftily.

Boba scowled. Then, unexpectedly, he laughed. "Me neither."

Ygabba smiled. The other children crowded behind them, laughing excitedly and hushing one another.

"I have to leave you now," Ygabba said.

She gestured at the children. They nodded. Then, breaking into groups of twos and threes, they ran across the crowded street. In seconds they had all disappeared, like ants into an ant hill.

Only Boba and Ygabba remained.

"Well," Ygabba said. She stuck out a dirty hand.

Boba hesitated. He looked down to see if there was an eye in her palm. There wasn't. He grinned and took her hand.

"Good luck," said Ygabba.

"Thanks," said Boba. "I'll need it."

With a smile, Ygabba turned and began to spring across the road. Halfway across she stopped.

"Hey — I never asked," she called back to him. "What's your name?"

"Boba," he said. "Boba Fett."

"Boba Fett," the girl repeated. She smiled broadly. "That's a name I'll remember!"

"I sure hope so," said Boba. He slipped the helmet over his head and watched as Ygabba was swallowed by the crowd.

CHAPTER NINE

It was almost dark by the time he found his way to the southeast gate. The arena was vast, nearly a small city in itself. It seemed like Boba was on his own again.

He passed encampments of beggars, and bright-colored tents where gamblers sat and beckoned him to come inside. He saw a troop of firetalkers, and a trio of Gamorrean guards who took turns bashing each other with a club. Weatherbeaten water prospectors pushed their way to the arena, eager to gamble away what little wealth they had. Vendors sold water in small containers.

"Only ten dataries!" one called to Boba. "Cheapest price at the arena!"

"No thanks," muttered Boba. His tongue felt like a rock in his mouth, swollen and dry.

He'd better earn some credits soon. *Really* soon.

Overhead floated yellow balloon cameras. They

would broadcast tonight's race to those who could not afford to watch it in person.

Like me, thought Boba.

But he didn't waste time thinking about that. He had a more important mission.

Find Jabba.

He kept walking. Beneath the northwest gate, there was a squadron of heavily armed droids. They were guarding a huge mobile warehouse. Boba wondered if this could be the weapons shipment Libkath had mentioned. If it was, how could a bunch of starved kids ever hope to steal its contents?

Well, he thought, *hunger is a good motivator. Just like thirst.*

His own stomach growled. Boba tried not to think about food. He hurried past the droids.

Overhead, the sky was quickly growing dark, swirled with purple and deep blue. Tatooine's twin suns hung low upon the horizon, an angry red. They reminded Boba of Master Libkath's eyes.

There were other eyes watching him, too. Beggars and aliens selling smuggled goods — crystals from k'Farri, Magravian cat-spice, cheap generators. Boba knew better than to listen to their harsh voices, or to those who tried to lure him into the gambling tents.

"Authorized Hutt crediteers! High stakes only!"

Boba stopped. He turned and saw a very large dome-shaped tent. It could easily have hidden *Slave I,* and another ship besides. As Boba watched, its door flap opened to let someone out. A cold, white burst of cloud followed. Boba took a step closer, enjoying the feel of the chill air against his skin.

"You!"

A tall, thin Etti towered above him. He was expensively dressed, and clutched a handful of blinking chips.

"No beggars here!" he said, and lashed out at Boba.

"I'm not a beggar," Boba said angrily, turning.

"No?" The Etti gamemaster looked down at him. He took note of the Mandalorian helmet. "No, I suppose not."

He gave Boba a mirthless smile. From the domed tent behind him came the sounds of deep, unsettling laughter. "But you're still not wanted here. Kurjj, get rid of this creature! Whoever he is. Bib Fortuna informs me that the chief wishes to observe the races from here this evening. He wishes *privacy,*" the Etti hissed, staring at Boba.

A hulking Drovian guard stepped out of the dome.

Boba swallowed, but stood his ground. "I'm looking for someone," he said.

The Drovian's huge hand reached for him. Still Boba did not flinch. The Etti stared. His cold smile grew wider. He watched as the Drovian started to grasp Boba's shoulder.

"Wait." The Etti raised his long thin arm. The Drovian guard grew still. The gambling master turned and fixed his glittering eyes on Boba.

"Were you sent by someone?" he asked slyly. He slid the chips into a pocket of his robe and rubbed his twiglike hands together. "Your employer has business with me, perhaps?"

Boba shook his head. "No," he said. His heart was pounding, but he was not afraid. "I represent myself alone."

"Indeed. And you are looking for . . . ?"

Boba took a deep breath. "I have business with Jabba the Hutt."

"Really?" The Etti's thin eyes creased with amusement. His voice rose, and he held open the tent flap behind him. "And what would a Mandalorian want with Jabba the Hutt?"

"That's my business," said Boba defiantly. He turned and started to walk away.

"HO HO HO!"

From the tent echoed a low, booming laugh, so

deep it seemed to make the ground shake beneath Boba's feet. "Business! I am always ready to do business — for a price! Bring him in, Kurjj!" a voice called in Huttese, which Boba could understand.

Boba froze.

That voice could belong to only one being on Tatooine. One being in the entire galaxy.

"He says he has business with Jabba the Hutt?" the voice roared. "Well then, it's time we met!"

CHAPTER TEN

With a nasty smile, the Etti held the tent flap open. The Drovian pushed Boba roughly inside.

Boba looked up.

Ulp, he thought. *This looks bad.*

He had never been more grateful for his father's battle helmet. He only prayed that the thing before him couldn't see him inside it.

When Boba first met Count Dooku, he thought the tall, elegant man was sinister, but not truly frightening. As for Aurra Sing — she was powerful and cunning, and absolutely ruthless.

But she was a bounty hunter, like Boba. He could understand how she thought. He could understand how she would react, and sometimes even predict it.

But this — *thing* — in front of him almost defied understanding.

Part of it was simply how huge he was. Back on

Aargau, Boba had glimpsed Jabba's nephew, Gorga the Hutt. Gorga had been big and disgusting.

But he was nothing compared to his uncle Jabba.

Jabba wasn't merely big. He was immense.

And he was hideous.

His mounded, sluglike form nearly filled the great dome of the tent. He reclined on a wide raised platform covered with beautiful handwoven rugs and tapestries, all coated with thick slime.

Jabba's followers occupied every remaining bit of space. Some of them were watching a Podrace on a large viewscreen. Others were hunched over gambling tables. Still others sat silently, moving chips and jewels back and forth in complex games of chance. Boba counted numerous guards, Drovians as well as the hulking Gamorrean guards preferred by the Hutt clan.

In addition to security, there was a large group of entertainers and athletes — jugglers, dancers, Podracers, acrobats — as well as Jabba's "pets." These were creatures nearly as ugly and threatening as the great Hutt himself. Most of them were in cages that hung from the domed ceiling. Boba nervously eyed a dwarf vornskr crouched near the entry, its whiplike tail lashing and its razor teeth exposed in a wicked grin.

The miniature vornskr snarled menacingly. Boba took this as his cue to introduce himself.

He said, in Huttese, "Jabba — er, sir. I am an emissary from Jango Fett."

Atop his mound of swollen flesh, Jabba's huge head slowly turned. He regarded Boba coolly with almond-shaped, amber eyes. His froglike tongue flicked in and out of a lipless mouth.

I bet there are planets smaller than he is, Boba thought. He forced himself to stare brazenly at the looming crime lord.

"Well, well!" Jabba rumbled. He gazed down at Boba with amused disdain. "What have we here? Another volunteer for the races tonight? I don't need another pilot. Not unless one of them dies on the finish line. HO! HO! HO!"

His body shook with laughter. Jabba's lackeys laughed, too. Boba thought their amusement sounded much more forced than the Hutt's.

"I'm not here for the race," Boba said. From inside his helmet, he saw several gamblers glance up from their tables. "I have come —"

He hesitated.

Why *had* he come?

For knowledge you must find Jabba.

Well, he'd certainly found Jabba! Boba looked up to see those evil narrow eyes staring at him.

"I — I have come to offer my services to you, O Great One," said Boba.

Peals of laughter shook the dome. Even the vornskr howled gleefully. Only Jabba continued to gaze at Boba, and said nothing.

"His services!" roared a Noghri pilot.

A lithe Carratosian pirate eyed Boba and snickered.

"Maybe he can clean up after the vornskr," she suggested.

Boba clenched his fists as the Gamorrean boars punched each other and guffawed.

"SILENCE!" thundered Jabba.

Immediately the dome grew still. Boba could no longer hear the click of gaming pieces; nothing but his own breath moving in and out of the helmet.

One of Jabba's too-small arms punched at the air. "What is so amusing?" he boomed in Huttese. "Who feels his own services are so important? YOU?"

Jabba turned and stared at the Carratosian. His long pale tongue oozed from his mouth. "Perhaps YOU are disposable, eh?"

"N-no sir," she stammered. "I only meant —"

Without warning, Jabba's powerful tail slashed across the floor. It struck her and she went sprawling.

"Insolent!" he cried. He turned to stare once more at Boba. "You, too, are insolent! No one approaches me without proper introduction."

"I didn't know," Boba said. "I —"

"Ignorance is no excuse!" roared Jabba. "And the penalty for ignorance is — death!"

CHAPTER ELEVEN

Death.

Boba thought fast. Then he spoke fast.

"Jabba — Mightiest of Hutts!" he cried. He was careful to face Jabba directly, and to show no fear.

"It is precisely my ignorance that has brought me here!" Boba continued. "'For knowledge you must seek out Jabba the Hutt' — that is what Jango Fett told me. That is why I have come to you."

Jabba stared at him. "For knowledge, eh?"

He sounded pleased. Boba drew a breath of relief.

"Do you hear that?" Jabba boomed, turning to his army of lackeys. "This stranger has come to me for knowledge! For this he has risked death, torture, and enslavement!"

Uh-oh, thought Boba.

Jabba turned back at him. "Well, intruder! You have come for a good reason. I know very much!"

The sluglike Hutt glanced at the monitor show-ing a Podrace. He gave a long, rumbling laugh. "Some might say I know what will happen *before* it happens."

Uneasy laughter rang out from the others in the room. Jabba leaned forward, peering at Boba with cunning eyes.

"You say that Jango Fett sent you? I had heard that he was dead. Killed by the Jedi on Geonosis. Is this true?"

Once again Boba was glad the helmet hid his face.

"Yes," he said. The word came out almost as a gasp. "Yes, it is true."

"I know of Jango's skill. He was courageous, and a man of his word. He was one of the finest bounty hunters in the galaxy."

"Some might say the very finest," interjected Boba without thinking

"Hmmmm." Jabba's eyes narrowed. "You, too, Mandalorian intruder, seem to have courage. But you have broken a rule by coming here. So I will give you a choice."

Jabba's flabby arm gestured at the viewscreen. Nearly everyone inside the dome was now clus-tered in front of it, eagerly watching a Podrace. "Tell me who you think will win this race. If you are correct, I will take you with me to my B'omarrian Palace. There you will serve me."

Boba nodded. "Thank you," he began, but Jabba raised a hand to cut him off.

"If you are wrong, you will still accompany me to my palace — but you will not serve me. Instead you will be *served* — to one of my pit beasts!"

CHAPTER TWELVE

Boba turned to stare at the monitor. Numbers and words scrolled across the bottom of the viewscreen. Statistics, the names of this evening's Podracers, their homeworlds, and racing class. Then the image changed. Boba saw the inside of the huge arena, packed with shouting, cheering, waving viewers.

I wonder if Ygabba's in there somewhere, Boba thought. *I wonder if she ever found the weapons shipment.*

But he couldn't wonder for long.

"Three more minutes!" shouted Estral, the gamemaster. "All bets must be in!"

Sleek machines flashed across the viewscreen — the Podracers. Boba watched them eagerly.

Man, I'd love to get my hands on one of those!

High-combustion engines made it possible for the Podracers to reach speeds of eight hundred kilometers an hour. Pit droids scrambled around the vehicles. They adjusted fuel levels and made last-minute repairs. Boba would have been glad to pilot any one of the racers — but which one was going to win tonight?

"Two more minutes!" cried the Etti.

Boba angled closer to the viewscreen. Now it showed profiles of the various racers. Boba recognized a few of them — the dinosaurian Chros-filik of Phu; Gasgano; Ody Mandrell; LobwuWa Loba, a thuggish Aqualish who seemed to be a local favorite; the eager young Aleena, Mab Kador, in his retrofitted *White Panther.*

But there were others, too, names and faces Boba had never seen before. How could he possibly choose the one who would beat the rest? Humans and aliens alike were massed inside the arena, making bets. Many of them would lose their life fortunes before the night was through. A few would probably lose their lives.

Boba didn't want to be one of them.

Despite the cool air inside the dome, a trickle of sweat began to inch down Boba's neck. His shoulder hurt where the helmet chafed his skin. He rubbed it gingerly, thinking hard. Jabba's guests crowded around the Etti gamemaster, shoving credits into his long thin hands.

"One minute!" he cried.

From the corner of his eye, Boba saw Jabba watching him. Quickly the young bounty hunter looked back at the viewscreen.

The statistics showed that Mab Kador had been undefeated for the last three races. *He looks young and hungry,* Boba thought, *and he has a great Podracer. That's who I'd back. That's who I'd want to win.*

But was that who Jabba was backing in the race? Boba had heard that the criminal overlord controlled everything on Tatooine, from blaster smuggling to the import of illegal spices. Every gambling den was under Hutt supervision. Every petty criminal paid tribute to Jabba. So did every rising crime lord. Those who grew too ambitious, those who tried to double-cross Jabba, were sought out by bounty hunters and brought to Jabba's palace.

Even on remote Kamino, Boba had heard horrible stories of what happened inside the fortress of Jabba the Hutt. He had never thought he might see it for himself.

"Twenty seconds!"

Boba swallowed. His hand slid into his pocket and touched his father's book. He didn't dare take it out, but just feeling it reassured him a little.

For knowledge you must find Jabba. He will not give it; you must take it.

"Time's up!"

Boba let his breath out. When he lifted his head, he saw Jabba gazing at him with those wicked, serpentlike eyes.

"So, young Mandalorian! Have you made your choice?"

Everyone inside the dome crowded in front of the viewscreen — everyone except for Boba and Jabba the Hutt. The gangster's pale tongue flicked from his mouth. He reached into a large basket overflowing with Ylesian white worms, grabbed a handful of squirming grubs, and shoved them into his mouth. Boba felt sick. From the viewscreen came the roar of the arena's crowd as the signal was given.

The race had started.

"Tell me — now!" roared Jabba. "You said you came to me for knowledge? You must show that you yourself possess it! *Who will be the winner?*"

Boba stared at the crime lord.

He will not give it; you must take it.

And suddenly, he knew the right answer.

CHAPTER THIRTEEN

"Well?" demanded Jabba.

Fearlessly, Boba looked at him. "O wisest of Hutts! The winner will be — whoever you want it to be!"

Inside the dome everything abruptly grew silent, except for the muted viewscreen. From outside, Boba could hear a wave of sound, shouts, and cheers echoing from the arena. There was the muffled explosion of a blaster. On his raised throne, Jabba stared down at Boba Fett. Very slowly he raised his flabby arms. His eyes narrowed. His entire vast body began to shake. His long, fat tail rippled and coiled like a dying slug.

Jabba the Hutt was laughing.

"HO HO!" The entire dome shook as he bellowed and roared. "Well said, young warrior!" He grabbed another fistful of worms and crammed them into his mouth, without ceasing to speak. "A clever answer! And a true one!"

Inside his helmet, Boba sighed with relief.

"Thank you, O Great and Wise Hutt," he said. He tipped his head respectfully. It was a good thing Jabba couldn't see his face! "I am overwhelmed."

Overwhelmed with disgust, Boba added to himself.

"Estral!" boomed Jabba. His flailing arm beckoned to the Etti gamemaster. "Collect their credits! We're leaving!"

Boba looked around, confused.

"But the race isn't over," he blurted.

Once more Jabba heaved with laughter. "I know who will win. I have more important business to attend to."

He leaned forward, staring intently at Boba. "Young Mandalorian! You said you were sent by Jango Fett."

Boba nodded. "That's right."

"So you, too, are a bounty hunter?"

Boba's voice was loud and clear. "Yes. I am."

"That is good. I am always in need of bounty hunters — even small ones. You will come with me to my palace. My major-domo, Bib Fortuna, will arrange for you to be outfitted there. Until you have discharged your debt to me, you will be under my command."

"My debt to you?" Boba said. He couldn't keep outrage from his voice. "What do I owe you for?"

Immediately he felt the hot breath of the Drovian guard upon his neck.

"You will die for that," the Drovian grunted.

He drew a curved litch-knife from his belt and held it just inches from Boba's face.

"And," the Drovian added with a twisted smile, "you will die slowly."

CHAPTER FOURTEEN

Boba had no time to think. He acted.

Without a sound he leaped to one side. The Drovian's knife whistled harmlessly through the air where, a nanosecond before, Boba had been.

"Huh?" gaped the hulking alien.

A small table stood near the viewscreen. Boba grabbed the table and swung it in front of him, fending off the Drovian's blade. Jabba's guests yelled and scattered in all directions. Jabba himself watched, laughing coarsely.

"You will pay for this!" croaked the Drovian.

As the guard bore down on him, Boba thrust the table upward. The knife stuck in the wood surface. While the Drovian struggled to free his weapon, Boba pushed the table up farther. Then he darted sideways, kicking at the lumbering guard's knees. With a groaning thud, the Drovian stumbled and fell. Jabba's guests laughed as Boba turned to breathlessly face Jabba.

"I am no one's slave or servant!" Boba said. "I will work for you, for a price — but I will name that price!"

Jabba's laughter stilled. He gazed at Boba. After a moment he nodded. "You are my kind of scum! You will make a good hunter."

The protection of his helmet made Boba feel bold. "Who's to say I'm not one already?"

Jabba smiled slyly. "Soon you will have the chance to prove it. I have a job that needs to be executed. I have already contacted another hunter, but perhaps the assignment should be yours."

Jabba turned and gave a disdainful glance at the Drovian. "Bring him back to the palace," he ordered his guards. "Once we have arrived, put him in the holding pen."

The Drovian roared and fought furiously as the Gamorreans grabbed him and led him away.

Boba watched them go. He had never imagined it would be possible to feel pity for a Drovian. Still, the thought of Jabba's pit beasts made him hope that the gangster might change his mind.

"Estral!" boomed Jabba. "I have commanded Bib Fortuna to ready the sail barge for our departure. We leave immediately. Ensure that this dome is dismantled. And see that our new recruit is not left behind."

"Yes, m'lord," replied the Etti.

He turned and looked at Boba. It was obvious that he was not impressed by what he saw. "The sail barge will be here in a few minutes. You can park your speeder in the holding area. Food will be served on the main deck after departure."

Boba said, "I have no speeder."

"A bounty hunter without a vehicle?" asked Estral with contempt.

"My ship's being overhauled," Boba added quickly. "It's in Mentis Qinx's docking bay."

Estral fixed him with a cold smile. "Qinx extends much credit to those in need. In exchange he demands huge fees. Many find they are unable to pay, and he keeps their vessels. Jabba the Hutt will own you before you get your ship back."

"We'll see about that," snapped Boba.

But behind the helmet, his face fell. Being a bounty hunter meant having the freedom to live and travel where he wanted to, when he wanted to.

He did not want to have to answer to Jabba the Hutt forever.

He did not want to answer to anyone but himself.

Still, Estral was right. Boba needed credits to pay for the repairs and refueling of *Slave I*. Jabba had said he needed bounty hunters. He said he had a job that needed to be executed. If Boba did that job, he could demand enough credits — and more — to reclaim his ship. He could set out on his own then, and go anywhere in the galaxy.

He would be free.

Even better.

At long last, he would be a bounty hunter.

CHAPTER FIFTEEN

Months before, Boba had been on the Republic Troopship *Candaserri*, a ship so big it was almost like a small planet.

Jabba the Hutt's sail barge was not that big, but it was big enough. Looking at it made Boba feel as though he was gazing at a small city within a city. A world within a world.

It was dark now, but there were enough bright lights around the arena to throw shadows everywhere. After Jabba was escorted from the dome, Boba and the rest went outside. The barge hovered above the ground. Bib Fortuna, Jabba's major-domo, commanded gangplanks and ladders to be deployed. Slaves and servants ran up and down, readying the barge for departure.

"Hurry!" hissed Fortuna.

Once Jabba was aboard, he would be impatient to leave. It was not a good idea to make him wait!

Boba wandered a few meters away from the

barge. He'd sneaked a sip of water to drink inside the dome, and a few dried ninchifs, tiny cavefish no bigger than his fingernail. He couldn't remember the last time he'd had a full meal.

He pushed that thought aside and crouched on the ground. There he watched Jabba's servants deflate the portable dome, like a great balloon.

It took only minutes. More servants scurried down from the sail barge, gathering the dome's contents. Gambling equipment and furniture was carted off. It would be stored in the vessel's cargo bays during the journey to Jabba's palace.

Jabba's palace. Boba had heard rumors about that place.

What he heard wasn't good. Not at all.

And now that he'd seen Jabba in the flesh, Boba was pretty sure the palace would be even worse than the rumors. He had better be ready for anything.

He leaned back and adjusted his helmet. He switched on the infrared vision feature. Immediately everything around him was shrouded in black and red.

"Ugh!" said Boba, grimacing.

Now he could see all of Tatooine's nighttime vermin. Sandrats scurried everywhere, feeding on trash left by arena goers. Sandscorpions scuttled from rock to rock, their pincers held high.

Boba saw several small figures creep from the shadows, unheeded. They snatched a metal crate and were gone in an instant.

Libkath's army at work, he thought with grudging respect.

"You look pretty happy," a low voice said behind him.

Boba whirled. "Ygabba!"

Behind him stood a slender figure clad in rags. "Got it in one," she said, and smiled. With one dirty hand she touched the edge of his helmet. "Huh. I think I liked you better without that. Aren't you hot in there?"

"Yeah. And thirsty."

Ygabba moved to crouch beside him. "Well, I can help you with that, at least. Here —"

She held out a small container of water. Boba looked at her, then took it gratefully. He glanced around to make sure no one else was watching. Then he pushed up his helmet and gulped the water.

It smelled strongly of dust and purification chemicals. There were bits of grit and sand in it. It was way too warm.

It was the best water he had ever tasted.

"Thank you," he said when the last drop was gone. He handed the container back to her, and lowered his helmet's visor. "Did you find what you were looking for?"

She nodded. "We did. All those droids guarding that tank back there? That was just a decoy. The real shipment was hidden with a shipment of water from a moisture farm near Bestine. That's where this came from," she added, holding up the empty container. "To tell you the truth, I'd rather have taken the water."

"But you got the weapons?"

Ygabba smiled. "Of course." Then her smile faded. "We have no choice. If we don't do as Libkath orders, bad things happen."

"What kind of bad things?"

"Kids disappear. We never see them again. Libkath sells them as slaves or indentured servants. Or worse."

Her expression darkened. Boba thought of how bad off Ygabba and the others seemed now. If something was worse than that, it must be really, *really* bad.

"Where do the weapons go?" he asked.

Ygabba shrugged. "Smuggling is big business

on Tatooine. Some people say it's the only business. There are a lot of people who want weapons."

Boba thought for a moment. "So you're saying
these weapons were smuggled here in the first
place. Now Libkath is double-crossing whoever
smuggled them in, by stealing them?"

"That's right. And the only reason he gets away
with it is that no one suspects us. Like I said before. Grown-ups never take us seriously. Until they
catch us."

Suddenly she got up. "Well, I better get going. I
have to meet the others."

Boba said, "Ygabba, wait."

She stopped. "What?"

"Why don't you just escape? I mean, Tatooine is
a big planet. Libkath couldn't track you all down if
you all ran away. And you said the toxin wouldn't be
released unless you left the planet."

"True." She shook her head sadly. "But the little
ones are too small. They could never keep up with
the rest of us."

"But you could go for help," said Boba. "Someone would have to listen. Someone would have to
help."

Ygabba's eyes brimmed with tears. "We have
no families, and for those of us who still have rela-

tives, he threatens to kill them if we ever go home. Life is hard enough for them here on Tatooine. We can survive in Mos Espa. Someday, when we're older, we will find our way back home. I don't know how. But we will."

Boba stared at her. He nodded. "I think you're brave, Ygabba. If there's some way I can help you and the others, I will."

Ygabba looked at him. She smiled. "Thanks, Boba."

She glanced up at the sail barge. Its banners were being unfurled. The airsailing crew was pulling up lines and getting ready to leave.

"Looks like you found what you were looking for, too," she said.

Boba stood beside her. "Yes. Jabba agreed to take me on — as a bounty hunter!"

He couldn't keep the pride from his voice.

Ygabba looked at him. Slowly, she smiled. "Boba Fett, bounty hunter! I definitely won't forget that."

"No. And I won't forget all of you, either."

From the sail barge came the fanfare of a trumpet. Jabba the Hutt was ready to depart.

"Good-bye, Ygabba!" Boba called as he ran to the barge. He grabbed a rope ladder and quickly climbed it, swinging himself on board. Rough hands grabbed him and pushed him onto the deck.

"Get below!" a Gamorrean guard shouted at him. "No riffraff where Jabba can see you!"

"I've been invited by Jabba," Boba protested. "As a bounty hunter —"

Harsh laughter came from the guard. "Get below with the other hired guns!" he brayed, and shoved Boba toward a door.

"You —!" Boba started to shout. Then he thought better of it. He gave one last look out toward the arena. A small figure stood where the dome had been, watching him.

"Go'wan!"

A huge gnarled hand shoved Boba through the door into the darkness of Jabba's barge.

CHAPTER SIXTEEN

On the upper deck, Jabba and his invited guests drank and ate. Music played. Acrobats tumbled and Twi'lek dancers leaped and turned. The barge's sails filled with air, as the great vessel came about and sailed majestically above the ground, heading for the Western Dune Sea. Overhead, stars burned through a sky black as Hapes velvet. The air smelled of roasting meat, of sweet, cool fruit sherbets, of flowers imported at fabulous expense from distant green worlds. A Mrlssi harpist played and sang while Jabba sat on his throne and crammed handfuls of writhing worms into his mouth. Jabba's guests wandered across the deck. They gazed out at the starlit desert beneath them, laughing and scheming and drinking Jabba's fine Chandrilan wines.

Unfortunately, Boba had only a glimpse of all of this splendor. He could only hear the music and merriment, and smell the mouth-watering odors of rare meats and fruits.

He was in the hold beneath the upper deck. There were no stars here to light the darkness. The space was dimly lit by swaying light globes suspended from the ceiling. There was no food or water. The air was close and hot, and stank of dirty straw and penned beasts. Off-duty crew members milled about, cursing and gambling away their pay. Some slept in hammocks slung along the walls. A few amused themselves by poking sticks into cages that held new pit beasts bound for Jabba's palace.

Boba picked his way carefully through the crowded space. He paused to look into a cage holding a Gallion tripion. The immense scorpionlike creature clashed its claws. Its poison-tipped tail clattered against the bars of its cage as a guard poked his sword through the slats.

"You'll be fed soon enough!" he sneered as his comrades laughed.

One of them looked at Boba. "Another newcomer?" His face creased in a leering smile. "That'll be the third bounty hunter this month that Jabba's set after Gilramos!"

"Gilramos?" asked Boba.

"That's right! A regular thorn in Jabba's tail, that one is. And a hard thorn to dislodge. He killed the last two bounty hunters who came looking for him."

The guard looked Boba up and down. He laughed derisively. "Looks like you'll make it three," he said, and turned back to tormenting the tripion.

"Third time's the charm," Boba muttered. He crossed over to the wall, trying to keep his balance. The air barge moved swiftly — they would reach the palace by morning, he'd heard someone say.

But the air yacht didn't always move smoothly. Sometimes it would fall with a sickening jerk. Other times it would abruptly soar straight up, hundreds of meters into the air. When this happened, Boba was glad he couldn't see outside. He was also glad he hadn't eaten much. He would hate to get airsick!

"So you're another bounty hunter," someone announced. "Jabba must really be getting desperate."

A wizened old man approached Boba, who was not much shorter than he was. The old man wore a flowing green robe, covered with a long, stained apron. His sparse white hair was almost hidden beneath a white cap. His face was brown and wrinkled as a dried gorapple, but his blue eyes were kind.

"Ye-es," said Boba. He stared at the man distrustfully. "I was sent here by Jango Fett."

The man's eyes widened. "Jango Fett? I would keep that information private, if I were you. Durge will not be happy to hear it!"

Boba's stomach fell. "Durge?"

The man shook his head. "No more chatter — first things first. Who are you?"

Boba stiffened. He said nothing. After a moment the man extended his hand. He pointed to an alcove where a narrow berth had been carved into the wall.

"Come," he said kindly. "It is a long journey to Jabba's fortress. Not everyone in Jabba's employ is as unpleasant as these individuals —"

He gestured at the Gamorreans, now busy playing a game with knives.

"Most, perhaps," the old man added, "but not all. For example, me. My name is Gab'borah Hise. I am the dessert chef assigned to this sail barge."

Boba grinned. "There are others?"

"Oh, yes — many. Dozens of dessert chefs alone! Jabba may dine upon those disgusting white worms, but his guests and his legion of gangsters have varied appetites. Their taste has become as depraved as Jabba's own, however. I must constantly think of new ways of tempting them with food."

Boba followed him to the alcove and sat down. Gab'borah sighed, smoothing the front of his apron.

"I did not always work for Jabba. Once, I was the head cook at a cantina in Mos Eisley. I was very successful. *Too* successful. Jabba heard how good I was. He made me an offer I could not refuse."

Boba smiled. "I understand. You had no choice but to come here."

"I had no choice," agreed the old man. "Once I cooked for smugglers and merchants. Now I cook for smugglers and gangsters. Earlier this evening I was preparing a most elegant confection. Stewed, flaming collypods with tangerette cream and figs. Absolutely delicious! Unfortunately, I served a sample to Bib Fortuna. One of the collypods, though in flames, was not quite dead. It burned his sleeve. Fortunately, I was able to put the flames out. Then I bribed Fortuna with a month's worth of wealth. I also gave him a Ziziibbon truffle, freshly made this morning. Bib Fortuna is quite fond of them."

Gab'borah shrugged. "So he did not throw me into a Sarlacc pit, as he would surely have done otherwise. But that is how I have come to be sent down here, in disgrace."

He slid a wrinkled hand into the pocket of his robe and withdrew a small, round object. It was bright green, threaded with red and yellow.

"Here." He held it out to Boba. "I saved this one. Don't worry, it's not poisoned," he said, and to prove it, took a little bite. "See? Try it. Tell me what you think."

Boba looked at it warily. Then he turned aside,

lifting his helmet a scant inch so that he could pop the truffle into his mouth.

It smelled delicious.

It *was* delicious.

"That's great!" Boba said thickly through a mouthful.

Gab'borah nodded. "I know. In all the galaxy, I alone have the recipe — another reason Bib Fortuna will never let me come to serious harm."

"Only you?" Boba licked his lips, savoring the last bit of sweetness.

"Yes." Gab'borah turned away. His withered face grew sad. "I was going to leave the secret with my only child and heir, but . . ."

His voice trailed off. In one of the cages, a vrblther gave its weird yodeling roar. Boba rubbed his eyes. It was late. He needed to sleep. But first he had a question for Gab'borah.

"You mentioned a name before. Durge." Boba made his voice sound casual. "Is he here?"

"Durge?" The old man suppressed a shudder. "A bounty hunter of terrible strength and destructive power."

He reached to touch Boba's helmet. "You should be very wary of him. Durge hates Mandalorians almost as much as he hates the Jedi. His body armor is tattooed with the symbols of Mandalorians he has slain."

"Now I remember," said Boba, pretending this was all new to him. He felt a chill, despite the hold's hot, musty air. "He wanted to be the source for the clone army."

Gab'borah looked at Boba with respect. "That is the rumor," he said. "How is it you come to know this?"

Boba hesitated. Then he said, "Jango Fett told me."

Gab'borah's eyes grew keen. "Then you know that Durge rejoiced when Jango Fett was killed. His only regret was that he was not the one to deal Jango Fett his death blow."

"Yes," Boba said. His eyes watered. He fought to keep his voice steady. "I know."

"You must also know then that your life will be in danger if Durge sees you."

"I have been hired by Jabba the Hutt to be his bounty hunter," Boba answered fiercely. "I am under his protection!"

Gab'borah shook his head. "Jabba has also hired Durge as his bounty hunter."

The chef grasped the side of the berth and stared out at the crowded, stuffy hold. The Gamorrean guards were sprawled on the floor or swung in hammocks, snoring loudly. Two stood as sentries by the ladder that led to the upper deck. Gab'borah looked at them, then turned back to Boba.

"Ah, young warrior," he said. "When it comes to Jabba the Hutt, there is no protection. There is no safety. There is only cunning and strength, if you are very, very lucky. And if you are not? Then there is only torment."

The old man stepped from the berth. He crawled into a hammock hanging beside it.

"We will be at the palace before many more hours have passed," he told Boba. "My advice to you now is to sleep. It is hard to be either cunning or strong if one is not well-rested."

Sleep! Boba stared at Gab'borah in disbelief. How could anyone sleep in a stinking, crowded place like this?

But in a few minutes, he found he was taking Gab'borah's advice.

It had been a very, very long day. At last, Boba slept.

CHAPTER SEVENTEEN

Boba woke to a low growling sound. When he opened his eyes, he saw the vrblther staring hungrily at him from inside its cage. Its green eyes glowed balefully. Its long yellow teeth showed between black gums. Boba hastily sat up in his berth. The vrblther's mouth opened in a grin as it lowered its head back onto its claws.

Now what? Boba looked around. The hold was quiet, except for the snores of the Gamorrean guards on the floor. Beside the ladder, the two sentries sat with their heads bowed.

Sleeping on the job! I bet Jabba wouldn't like that, thought Boba.

He glanced to where Gab'borah hung in his hammock, breathing heavily. Then Boba turned sideways in his berth, making sure no one could see him. He lifted his helmet.

Air! He couldn't really call it *fresh* air, but it sure beat breathing through the visor. Boba rubbed his eyes. Grit and sand stuck to his fingers. He wiped them on the tunic. Then he carefully removed his book.

He set it on his knees and opened it. Words glowed on the screen-page: *For knowledge you must find Jabba.*

Boba's finger hovered above the page. He touched a word.

Jabba.

Immediately the sentence faded and another screen appeared. Words filled it. Boba scanned them quickly, until he found what he was looking for.

Palace.

"Tell me," Boba whispered. He pressed the voiceover command. Immediately his father's voice began speaking to him. The voice was so low he had to strain to hear it.

"Jabba's palace is built upon what was once a B'omarr monastery. At all costs, avoid the lower levels. That is where the prisons and dungeons are, and the lairs of pit beasts that have escaped over the centuries. The uppermost level is where Jabba's most valued guests stay — as long as they *are* valued. The average guest ends up as a krayt's dinner. Or a Sarlaacs' lunch. Bounty hunters usually fare somewhat better, *if* they are successful."

The voice faded. Jango Fett's face filled the

screen, staring directly at Boba. "There is one rule, and one rule only, when dealing with Jabba the Hutt," his father's image pronounced solemnly. "*Do not fail.*"

"I won't fail," murmured Boba. His finger traced the outline of his father's face. For a second, Jango smiled at his son. Then the image disappeared, and the screen went blank. Boba saw his own reflection then. He didn't look like his father yet, but he wasn't the kid he used to be. His eyes had gotten fiercer. His mouth looked unaccustomed to smiling much.

Boba put the book away. He ran a hand through his hair by way of combing it, and stood. Light filtered through cracks in the barge walls. On the deck above he could hear footsteps and the clanging of a bell.

"Wake up, you slobs!" someone bellowed. A Gamorrean's twisted face appeared at the hatch atop the ladder. "We'll be docking in fifteen minutes!"

The sleeping guards groaned and grunted. They began stumbling to their feet, kicking at those still dozing on the floor. In his hammock Gab'borah stirred. He yawned, then clambered out, stretching.

"Morning already! I trust you slept soundly?" he asked Boba, and winked.

"Like a baby," Boba replied.

"That is good. Sleep is important for a warrior. And so is breakfast."

Gab'borah looked around stealthily. Then he pulled two small packets from his robe.

"Here," he whispered, giving one to Boba. "Gleb rations. Not as tasty as what you had last night, but it will fill your stomach and give you a day's worth of nutrients."

Boba unwrapped the package. Inside was a small flat bar of what looked like cardboard.

He sniffed it.

It smelled like cardboard. He looked curiously at Gab'borah, who was busily munching his rations. Boba shrugged and took a bite of his.

It *tasted* like cardboard, too. But it was better than nothing. Quickly he finished.

Just in time.

"You're wanted on deck!" A Gamorrean shoved a hairy fist at Gab'borah's stomach. The old man bowed and started hurrying for the ladder. Boba waited an instant, then started after him.

"Hey! No one said he wanted *you!*"

The beast grabbed Boba by the shoulder. In its cage, the vrblther let loose a warbling cry.

"He's getting hungry!" the Gamorrean said, his piggy eyes glinting with malice. "How's about we give him a little snack!"

Boba struggled against the guard. "I'm here at Jabba's request!" he shouted. "Let me go, or you'll pay!"

The guard sneered. "Jabba won't miss another bounty hunter — he's lost so many already!"

Boba landed a kick in the Gamorrean's stomach. With a roar of pain and rage the guard drew back, his fist raised. "Why, you —!"

"Excuse me." Gab'borah cleared his throat and gave the Gamorrean a cold look. "This warrior is here at Jabba's *special* request. And my own — he is to help prepare Jabba's morning repast."

The guard glared at the old man.

Gab'borah glared back. "I would not like to be the one responsible for making Jabba wait for his breakfast," he said. "Come—"

He beckoned for Boba. With a snarl the Gamorrean watched as Boba hurried to join the ancient chef.

"Are you really making Jabba's breakfast?" he whispered as he clambered up the hatch.

"No." Gab'borah stretched a hand out to pull Boba on deck. "He mostly eats those revolting white worms. And slimy little wuorls. But the Gamorreans are too stupid to remember that."

"Good thing," agreed Boba.

Gab'borah looked at Boba, his expression wistful.

"You are a courageous young man," he said. "And lucky. Many your own age here on Tatooine have disappeared. Kidnapped. Their families never hear from them again. Their fate is lost to us."

The old man's eyes grew sad. Gazing at him, Boba felt sad, too, but also excited.

"I saw them!" he began. "They —"

Before he could continue, the dark-robed figure of Bib Fortuna appeared.

"You!" he ordered in his thin voice. His clawed finger pointed at Gab'borah. "You are to proceed to the kitchens — immediately!"

Gab'borah bowed. "As you wish," he said to Bib Fortuna, then glanced at Boba. "I will proceed to the seventh kitchen," he murmured. "That is my customary place of employment."

Boba looked at him. He understood that this was the old man's way of telling him how he could be found.

"Good-bye," said Boba. Gab'borah smiled, then walked away. Bib Fortuna turned impatiently.

"And you —" The Twi'lek's orange eyes fixed on Boba. "*You* are to prepare for an audience with Jabba. Choose your words carefully," he added, his mouth twisting into a sneer. "They will probably be your last!"

CHAPTER EIGHTEEN

Boba watched as the Twi'lek headed for a raised area of the main deck. A brilliant yellow canopy billowed above it. Beneath the canopy, there was shade. There was shelter from Tatooine's twin suns, already burning fiercely with the dawn. There was a table laid out with food and pitchers of cool water, as valuable as precious metals on this desert planet.

And there was Jabba. He reclined upon a platform, one stubby hand grasping a froglike wuorl. With a groan of pleasure he plopped the wuorl into his mouth. Boba took a deep breath. He adjusted his helmet, then strode over

"O Exalted Hutt," he said. His voice was confident yet respectful. "I await your orders."

Jabba chewed noisily. He swallowed. He belched.

"You say you are a bounty hunter?" he asked.

"Yes, O Mighty Jabba."

Jabba stared at Boba's helmet. Boba felt a trickle of sweat on the back of his neck. He was glad that Jabba could not see his face. . . .

Or could he . . . ?

"You are small for a Mandalorian warrior," Jabba said slowly in Huttese. His eyes narrowed. "I have a task that is dangerous. It demands courage and skill."

"I have both," Boba pronounced.

"Others have said the same." Jabba shook with a spasm of laughter. "Their bones now lie in an acklay's den!"

"Excuse me, Exalted One." Bib Fortuna stepped onto the platform beside the gangster. He lowered his head and announced, "We have arrived at the palace."

Even as he spoke, the smooth motion of the sail barge stopped. Beneath Boba's feet the deck seemed to lurch. He caught his balance in time to keep from falling.

"O Great Jabba," he began. "I would like to —"

"Silence!" roared Jabba. He glared at Boba. "In five minutes I will meet with you and another bounty hunter in my throne room. There I will give you your assignment. If you are late, other arrangements will be made."

The crime lord gave a long, jeering laugh.

"These arrangements will involve my combat arachnids. They have not been fed for several days. I find
they fight better when they are hungry."

Boba nodded earnestly. "I won't be late," he
said.

But Jabba was already leaving.

The deck was in chaos. People hurried to raise
and lower ladders and planks. A wide ramp was in
place for Jabba's departure.

"Move it!" shouted a guard.

Boba hurried to the rail, shading his eyes from
the blazing suns. He stared out. For the first time,
he saw Jabba's palace.

"Wow!" he breathed.

Around him stretched the desolation of the
Dune Sea. Distant mountains loomed above shift-
ing red sands and deep canyons. Far, far away, tiny
black forms moved across the desert — a herd of
wild banthas.

Somewhere out there lived the barbarian Sand
People, the Tusken Raiders. Somewhere Jawas
scavenged space freighters and abandoned moisture farms.

But there were no Sand People here. There
were no Jawas.

This was the stronghold of Jabba the Hutt.

It was a fortress more huge and more strangely

beautiful than anything Boba had ever seen. An immense central tower rose from the desert cliffs, as tall as a mountain. Around it, slender spires and mushroom-shaped turrets cast purple shadows on the bright sand. Speeders flashed beneath them, carrying supplies and guests.

"It is impressive, is it not?" a robotic voice remarked.

Boba turned to see a humanoid PD protocol droid beside him. Its yellow plasteel body gleamed in the morning sun.

"Yes, it is," replied Boba. He adjusted his helmet to shade his eyes from the brilliance.

"Long, long ago it was a B'omarr monastery," the droid went on. "There were many thousands of monks here then. Now there are only a few. Their brains have been transferred into spider-droid casings. One can sometimes glimpse them on the upper levels."

Inside his helmet, Boba grimaced. *Ugh!* he thought. *Remind me not to go on the upper levels!*

"Keep moving!" a Gamorrean bellowed.

Boba eased himself toward a crowded ramp. The droid walked beside him. As they jostled their way onto the ramp, a deafening roar blasted through the calm desert air.

"Whoa!" exclaimed Boba. "What's that?"

He looked up. A large speeder thundered past. Blazing vapor trailed behind it. A tall, powerful figure straddled the speeder. Weapons bulged from the shoulders of his armor. Above his huge hands, grenades glittered like crystal eyes.

The speeder raced toward Jabba's citadel. Boba glimpsed the outline of a Mandalorian skull symbol glowing red against silvery armor.

"That is Durge," said the droid. "Jabba heard he was on Tatooine and made him a large offer."

The droid gazed at Boba. Its round eyes were empty of emotion.

"Whoever fails will be given to Durge as a reward," the droid continued. "That is how he keeps his reflexes keen. He practices upon living prey. That is why he is the greatest bounty hunter here."

Boba stared back into the droid's eyes. He shook his head. "Durge is the greatest bounty hunter?" he said, thinking of what his father might say. "Well, I think it's time for a change!"

Boba's words sounded braver than he felt. But the droid did not notice.

"Come," it said. Behind them, Gamorrean guards stood impatiently, their weapons drawn. "I will escort you to the throne room."

"Thanks," said Boba. "I've never been here before."

"Do not thank me," the droid said in its cold, mechanical voice. "I doubt that you will ever come here again."

Without a word, Boba followed the droid down the ramp and into the shadow of Jabba's fortress.

CHAPTER NINETEEN

The inside of the palace was dark and cool. Boba breathed deeply in relief.

"Boy, that's better!" he remarked to the droid.

But his relief did not last long. A large, spider-like form on long metal legs tiptoed past. What looked like its head was actually a clear globe filled with fluid. Inside the fluid floated what looked like a brain.

Boba stared at it. He said, "Is that a monk?"

"No," said the droid. It began to walk down a dim hall. "That is the last bounty hunter Jabba sent after Gilramos. What remains of him, anyway."

Boba watched the creature stalk toward the shadows. Then he hurried after the droid. Behind him the click of the spider-droid's legs faded into silence.

"Why hasn't anyone been able to capture Gilramos?" he asked.

"Tatooine is a very big planet," said the droid.

"A very desolate planet. There are many places to hide in the desert. One could spend a lifetime searching for an enemy and never find him."

"Is that where Gilramos is hiding?" asked Boba. "In the desert?"

"So the bounty hunters think. Here —"

The droid stopped. It motioned at a high, carved arch. "This is Jabba's throne room. I must leave you here."

It turned and left.

Boba watched it go. His heart felt like a rock in his chest. He looked at the archway.

Once he passed through, he would be at the center of Jabba's realm.

He would be at Jabba's mercy.

No! he thought. He put his hand into his pocket and touched the book there. Immediately he felt calmer.

Fear is energy.

That is what his father had taught him. If you contain your own fear, it becomes power.

And power makes you strong.

Boba drew a deep breath. He felt his heart pounding, but now it did not frighten him. He looked at the arch.

From inside, he could hear music. He could hear voices. He could hear shrill cries and deep, powerful laughter. He could hear a voice dry and merciless as a desert storm.

Jabba.

And Durge.

"Time to go to work," said Boba.

He walked inside.

The throne room was large. Flickering flames rose and fell inside tall lamps. Shadowy figures danced and leaped. Someone trilled on a flute. Boba could smell smoke.

And roasting food. Near Jabba's throne a spit turned. On it was a huge demon squid, its tentacles nicely browned. Boba lost his appetite.

"Bounty hunter!" Jabba shouted, a mountainous figure in the center of the room. "Approach!"

Boba stepped forward. "Your Huge Huttness," he said. He bowed. "I have come to receive your orders."

Boba looked up. On his throne, Jabba reclined. He watched Boba through slitted eyes. Around him, the dancers and singers stopped. They stared at Boba, too. Their eyes were round with fear.

And with anticipation.

"Did I ask you to speak?" roared Jabba. He leaned forward, his shadow falling across Boba.

"N-no," faltered Boba. "But —"

From Jabba's shadow another figure emerged. Huge and muscular, his silver body-armor shining.

It was Durge.

"Shall I destroy him now?" he cried. He raised his arm and pointed a blaster at Boba. On his chest the Mandalorian skull seemed to burn.

Boba tensed. From the corner of his eye he could see Jabba's guards, dozens of them. The doors were blocked.

He looked down. He could see a long groove in the floor.

A trapdoor. Jabba kept pit beasts for his depraved entertainment. And to punish those he was unhappy with. There would be no exit that way, either.

Boba glanced up. Beams crisscrossed the ceiling. Feline shooks were chained there, their tusks dripping. Their evil red eyes watched Boba hungrily.

Durge took a step toward Boba. "It will be my pleasure to kill you," he said, aiming his blaster.

"Your pleasure, perhaps!" boomed Jabba. "But not mine."

He gestured impatiently at Durge. The great bounty hunter continued to stare at Boba. Inside his battle helmet his eyes flickered crimson. Finally, he lowered his blaster. "If not now," he said, "then later."

"I have a task," continued Jabba the Hutt. "Someone has interfered with my smuggling trade.

Someone has refused to work with me. That someone must be killed."

"I will see to it!" said Boba. His voice echoed
loudly through the throne room.

"So you say." Jabba leaned back on his throne.
He extended his flabby hand. Immediately, a servant filled it with wriggling worms.

Jabba chewed the worms thoughtfully. He
pointed at Boba. He said, "Mandalorian, you have
no weapons!"

The bloated crime lord began to laugh. From
everywhere in the room more laughter rang out.

Only Durge was silent. He continued to stare at
Boba hatefully.

Boba shook his head. *Think fast!*

"That is so, O Exalted Jabba," he said quickly. "I
have waited to receive my arms from you, and you
alone. Because you are the greatest among your
kind. And I will be the greatest among bounty
hunters!"

Jabba smiled. "A good answer!"

Boba turned and stared fearlessly up at Durge.
"And a true one!"

The bounty hunter reached for his blaster. "You
will suffer great pain for that. I think it's time we
saw what's under your mask!"

With a roar, Durge lunged for him.

CHAPTER TWENTY

"Hoh hoh!" Jabba shook with delight. "Durge and an unarmed warrior!"

Boba wasted no time. Before Durge could catch him, Boba dove between his legs.

Jabba laughed, crying, "He is fast!"

"Not fast enough!" yelled Durge.

A flaming burst of red and orange shot from his weapon. Boba rolled. In an instant he was on his feet again. He looked around.

A few meters away was the spit. The squid dangled from it like a huge, empty glove. Fingers of flame ran up and down its tentacles.

Boba raced toward it, quick as a heartbeat. He grabbed one end of the spit. The metal was warm, but not hot. With a grunt he yanked it up, turning.

"You!" shouted Durge. One hand held a blaster, the other a dagger.

But all Boba saw was the Mandalorian skull

blazing on his chest. He gave a shout, then swung the long metal pole. The sizzling squid's tentacles fanned out like blades. They struck Durge in the face. For a moment he was blinded.

"Argh!"

But a moment was enough. Boba drove the metal pole at Durge's chest. The squid exploded into globs of burning fat, spattering Durge's face.

"That'll teach you!" yelled Boba. He turned, panting, to Jabba. "Now, if we could —"

"Not quite, Mandalorian!"

Boba darted to one side — but not fast enough. Something whistled toward him: Durge's blade. Boba ducked. He felt a glancing blow on his helmet. There was an instant of utter darkness. Then light and air poured like water across his face. Beside him he heard a sickening thump.

"What is this?" shouted Jabba in surprise. He heaved himself halfway from his throne. One plump hand pointed at the floor.

Boba blinked. He stared at the ground beside him —

Into the empty eyes of his battle helmet.

"He's only a boy!" shrilled one of Jabba's Twi'lek dancers. Her blue skin gleamed as she looked disdainfully at Durge. "The new bounty hunter is a boy!"

"A boy?" echoed Jabba. For a moment he was silent.

Boba froze. His hand reached for his helmet, but he didn't dare move. A few meters away, Durge also stood watching him, his goal of unmasking Boba accomplished.

Then Jabba began to laugh. "A boy! And he defeated Durge!"

"He will not live to manhood!" With a cry Durge started toward Boba.

"Stop!" roared Jabba. Immediately a dozen Gamorrean guards surrounded the bounty hunter. Durge raised his blaster.

Then more guards appeared. Reluctantly he holstered the weapon. The gaze he turned upon Boba held more fury and pure hatred than Boba had ever seen. When he spoke, it was in a low voice that only Boba could hear.

"I will hunt you down. That is my assignment, and I *never* leave an assignment unfinished."

Quickly Boba turned away. He picked up his helmet and held it beneath his arm. Then he looked up at the throne. He knew the crime lord was his best chance at protection.

"O Wise Jabba," he said. "Let me serve you. Arm me. Give me a speeder. Then tell me your bidding, and I will do it."

"Arm you?" Jabba's mouth split into a taunting smile. "But you have no need of arms! You have just shown us that! As for my bidding . . ."

The sluglike gangster looked from Boba to Durge. "Someone has interfered with my smuggling operation here on Tatooine. He has a ring of thieves who help him. They steal my weapon shipments. Then he sells the weapons."

"Who does he sell them to?" asked Boba.

"To the Separatists." Jabba leaned forward. "But I do not care who he sells them to. I care only that he has taken what is mine. I want him destroyed. I want his supporters killed as well."

Boba nodded. "Do you know his name?"

"Yes. He is a Neimoidian. His name is Gilramos Libkath."

"Gilramos *Libkath?*"repeated Boba in disbelief.

"That's what I said," replied Jabba impatiently. "Do you know of him?"

Libkath! That's the name Ygabba used— for the Master!

Boba hid his dismay. "Do I know of him?" he repeated.

Quickly he looked aside at Durge.

The hated bounty hunter was easily twice his size. Durge was armed. He had a speeder. He hated Mandalorians.

And, to judge from the way he stared at Boba, he hated Boba most of all.

I was lucky just now, Boba thought. *I've taken Durge by surprise — twice.*

He will never let that happen again.

Boba's hand tightened on his helmet.

My greatest strength right now is knowledge.

I know who Gilramos Libkath is. I know where he is.

Boba corrected himself. *Where he will be, when he arrives to take the weapons Ygabba and the others stole for him.*

"I asked you a question!" said Jabba. "Do you know of Gilramos Libkath?"

Boba hesitated. Then he shook his head. "No. But I will find him."

"Do not trust him!" Durge broke in. Around him the Gamorrean guards grunted under their breath. "He has deceived you once already! He will do so again!"

Durge thrust his fist toward Boba. "Give him to me, Jabba! I will make his lies die with him!"

Jabba regarded Durge thoughtfully. He turned to Boba. "He tells the truth. You deceived me — and those who deceive me do not live to speak of it."

"O Great Immensity! I did not deceive you," Boba replied. His voice was smooth and flattering.

"I could never deceive your great wisdom! I wanted only to show how ill prepared *this* bounty hunter was — by deceiving *him*."

He pointed at Durge. Jabba twisted to stare at him.

"Ah!" agreed the mighty gangster. He smiled. "Of course! I knew that!"

He gave a rolling laugh. Around him his lackeys tittered and sneered.

"Thank you, O Jabba." Boba looked at him boldly. "Now, if you give me new weapons, I will leave. I will not return until I have captured Gilramos Libkath."

"Give you weapons?" Jabba's voice turned cold. "I give nothing!"

He motioned to an alcove. Immediately Bib Fortuna stepped out from where he had been waiting. Jabba said, "These bounty hunters are wasting my time. They talk when they should act. This one" — Jabba pointed at Durge — "he has let a mere boy defeat him! His reflexes have grown slow." A sly smile creased Jabba's face. "Durge needs to sharpen his skills. Then he will hunt faster. He will hunt better."

"I will sharpen my teeth upon this boy's bones!" shouted Durge.

"Perhaps." Jabba shook his head. "But first you will meet several of my pit beasts."

Boba jolted backward as the ground beneath him trembled.

The trapdoor was opening!

"Combat arachnids!" squealed the Twi'lek dancer.

Murmurs of excitement filled the room. The Gamorrean guards shoved each other in expectation. Durge glared at Boba, then raised a fist defiantly at Jabba.

"I will best them!" he cried.

At their feet a wide gap appeared in the floor. Darkness filled it.

Darkness, and a chittering sound. As Boba stared, two immense Caridan combat arachnids clattered across the pit floor. Each had twelve legs, sharp and covered with razor spines. More spines covered their backs. Their mouths gaped open to reveal teeth like dripping daggers. Above their teeth, a dozen eyes glistened like poisonous jewels.

Boba sucked his breath in sharply. At the sound the arachnids swiveled. They stared up. Twenty-four spider eyes gazed at Boba unblinking.

"They are hungry," murmured Bib Fortuna. He smiled.

"As for you," Jabba looked at Boba. "Unless Durge's reflexes have gotten very, *very* slow, he will triumph."

"And then I will hunt," said Durge. His crimson eyes remained fixed on Boba. "I will hunt you!"

CHAPTER TWENTY-ONE

Boba fought a wave of fear. He looked at Jabba. "I have no weapons, O Great One —"

"Do you dare to argue with me?" roared Jabba. "You have a head start — a few minutes, if you are lucky. A few seconds, if you are not."

He gave a signal to the Gamorrean guards. They grabbed Durge. He resisted, but only a little; he wanted to fight. They dragged him to the edge of the floor. Below, the arachnids raised their legs threateningly. Their hungry mouths snapped open and shut.

"Drop him," said Jabba.

With grunts of pleasure, the guards shoved Durge into the pit. In the last instant before he fell, his eyes locked with Boba's.

"I will see you soon!" Durge shouted. "And it will be for the last time!"

The great bounty hunter dropped heavily to the

pit floor. His weapons were already raised, his eyes blazing.

The combat arachnids raced toward him. A ball of flame exploded from Durge's blaster.

Whatever else he is, thought Boba, *Durge is no coward.*

An ominous voice sounded in Boba's ear. "You are eager to join him?" Bib Fortuna asked.

"No thanks!" said Boba.

He backed away from the pit opening. On his throne, Jabba ate a fistful of worms. He belched, then looked at Boba.

"Perhaps you also need to sharpen your reflexes?"

Boba bowed hastily. "I will return — with Gilramos Libkath!" he said.

"Not just Gilramos," the gangster overlord warned. "I want his followers destroyed as well. *Every last one of them.*"

Boba's mouth went dry. He thought of Ygabba and the other children. He remembered the eerie glowing eyes on their palms. He remembered how tired they looked. How hungry.

How despairing, and how sad.

"I will deal with them, O Exalted One," said Boba.

And I will, too! he thought. *But Jabba doesn't need to know exactly how.*

Turning, he raced from the throne room.

"Now what?" Boba muttered to himself. *I know where Gilramos is, but how do I get there?*

He ran until he reached the end of a long hall-way. He stopped, panting, and looked around.

The hall divided into two passages. One passage was brightly lit. Cool air flowed from it. In the distance, Boba saw service droids and a Drovian servant waiting by a door.

He turned to the other passage. It was dark. The floor was rough.

But it smelled good. It smelled like food. It smelled like cooking.

"Gab'borah!"

"The seventh kitchen," the old man had said. *"That is my customary place of employment."*

Boba began to run down the dark passage. As he did, the smell of cooking grew stronger. After a minute, he came to an open door. He peered in-side.

It was a large kitchen. Steam filled the air. Huge pots bubbled on an open fireplace. An otterlike Selonian cook stood over the pots, stirring. He looked at Boba and frowned.

"Is this the seventh kitchen?" Boba gasped.

The Selonian shook his head. He dipped a long spoon into the pot. He lifted it, displaying a fat pink tube larva.

"This is the first kitchen," he said. He held the steaming grub toward Boba. "Care to taste?"

"Uh, not today!" said Boba.

He raced back into the hall. He glanced back down toward the main entry. He could see figures running back and forth. He heard shouting.

"Durge has already escaped," Boba said. "Man, he's fast — but I'm faster!"

He ran to the next door. Huge tanks filled with water lined the walls. Inside them, green and blue seafah shellfish crawled. Lambro sharks, another delicacy, swam restlessly back and forth.

"Kitchen seven?" Boba shouted at a droid dropping shellfish into a boiling cauldron.

"That way," the droid said, pointing farther on.

Back into the hall! The noise from the far end was louder now. Boba didn't waste time looking. He ran to the next door, then the next.

The third kitchen held vats of bubbling mugruebe stew. The smell was so good that Boba almost couldn't tear himself away.

But he had no trouble leaving the fourth room. It wasn't really a kitchen, but a breeding ground for white worms — millions of them. They squirmed and wriggled in long open trenches. Droids scooped up buckets of slimy worms and placed them on a conveyor belt.

"Yuck!" said Boba.

He would never be *that* hungry!

The fifth kitchen held only vegetables and fruits. Many of them were alive and still moving.

The sixth kitchen was devoted to meat. Boba stuck his head through the door. A Caridan cook waved a huge knife at him.

"Yes!" The oversized, roachlike alien grinned with excitement. "Finally! Our main course has arrived!"

"Wrong kitchen!" Boba yelled hastily.

He ran back into the hall. From the far end came shouts. He heard a deep voice he recognized as Durge's. He heard the loud explosive burst from a blaster.

He heard footsteps and an angry yell. They were very close.

Just ahead of Boba was the last door. Huttese letters and numerals were carved on it.

"This better be kitchen number seven," said Boba grimly.

He shoved the door open. Several men and women in Tatooine clothing stood around a long table. Strange objects covered it. They looked like brightly colored toys, or perhaps they were weapons? Boba couldn't tell.

But whatever they were, they smelled good.

No. They smelled *great*.

"Can I help you?" a woman asked.

Boba stood still. For a second he was dizzy. He breathed in the warm sugar, chocolate, scry-mint. He thought he might faint from hunger.

"Young sir!"

Boba blinked. In front of him was Gab'borah. The old man wore a bright green cook's robe and hat. One hand held a large spoon. The other grasped a wiggling eye-stalk. Its round blue eye peered at Boba.

"I'm putting the finishing touches on tonight's dessert," explained Gab'borah. He turned briskly and walked to the table. He bent and set the eye-stalk in the middle of one of the bright objects. It was not a toy or a weapon, Boba saw now. It was a cake.

"There!" said Gab'borah proudly. He beamed at Boba. "I'm so glad you came to visit me!"

From the hallway behind them came a sudden yell. Boba whirled. He yanked the door shut. He locked it.

"I need your help!" he gasped. "Now!"

The old man stared at him. An instant later he nodded.

"Go!" he said. He shooed away the other cooks. Then he looked at Boba again.

"What is it?" he asked in a low voice.

Another bellow came from behind the closed door. Gab'borah raised a knowing eyebrow.

"Ah — now I understand!" he said. "It is Durge. Jabba has set him loose on you."

"Right," said Boba. He looked around desperately. "Gab'borah, I need to get out of here fast. Not just out of this room. I need to get away from the entire fortress."

Gab'borah frowned. He and Boba glanced at the door. It was shaking. In a moment, Durge would burst through.

"Come with me," whispered the old man. He crossed the room, Boba at his heels. "Here —"

Gab'borah opened a door. Inside was a sort of closet, and another door. The closet was filled with junk.

Gab'borah muttered, "Now, I know it's here somewhere . . ."

The old man pawed through everything, searching. Old kitchen tools, bowls, and pans, discarded stove parts, cutlery . . .

And, hanging beside the door, a jet pack.

"Here it is!" Gab'borah grabbed the jet pack and handed it to Boba. "You see, I too am always thinking of escape!"

Boba examined the jet pack. It was an older model and designed for an adult. He looked at the fuel supply canisters.

"They're still full" he said. He looked gratefully at Gab'borah and grinned. "Thanks — this is great!"

"It is my pleasure," said the old man with a bow.

He watched as Boba adjusted the straps. Then Boba slung it onto his back. From the corridor came a deafening boom.

"Mandalorian runt!" a voice roared. Boba looked out in time to see Durge crash through the kitchen door.

"Go now!" cried Gab'borah. He pushed open the door inside the supply closet. He shoved Boba through it. "Quickly!"

"Whoa," exclaimed Boba.

He stood on a narrow space, hundreds of meters above the ground. Around him was the immensity of Jabba's fortress. Above, two orange suns burned and dazzled. Heat flashed down like toxic rain.

Below, so distant it was like a flaming mirage, stretched the Dune Sea.

"Out of my way, old man!" shouted Durge.

"Go!" cried Gab'borah as the huge bounty hunter pushed him aside.

Boba looked back. He didn't need any more urging. Just meters away, the murderous bounty hunter stood with his blaster aimed right at him.

"Now I've got you right where I want you!" Durge jeered. "Ready to die?"

"Not this time!" yelled Boba. He yanked his helmet over his face. He switched on the jet pack's ignition. Flame spurted behind him. Heat seared the back of his legs.

But Boba had no time to think about that. He had no time to think about anything.

"Whoooo — eeeeeee!" Boba yelled.

Beneath him the world fell away.

He was flying!

CHAPTER TWENTY-TWO

Boba had flown before, of course. He had flown in airspeeders and on swoop bikes. He had flown inside his hyperfast starship, *Slave I*.

But nothing was quite like this.

"Man, this is great!" he whooped as he somersaulted through the air. Jabba's palace was so small now it looked like one of Gab'borah's cakes. When Boba looked back, he could see Durge. The bounty hunter stood within the doorway leading into empty air. He was a shining speck no bigger than an insect. He was smaller than an insect.

Then he was gone!

Boba watched as the citadel disappeared into the landscape. Then he did a few more somersaults. He dove and swooped the way *Slave I* did through space, the way he had seen his own father swing through the air. He practiced steering the jet pack, remembering his father's movements, his father's way. He switched off the ignition and let his body go into freefall.

The ground raced to meet him, red and gold and black. At the last second, Boba switched the ignition back on. The fuel packs blazed and thundered. He pulled out of the dive. He soared back into the shimmering air. He spun a few more times, just for luck. Then he adjusted his helmet. He turned on its navigation program.

"Mos Espa," he commanded. Inside the helmet, red lights flickered to green. A stream of directional codes flashed before Boba's eyes. Then a virtual map shimmered across Boba's field of vision. He blinked.

It's too far away, he thought in dismay. A sailbarge might be able to get there in a day, but a jet pack?

Never.

Now what?

Boba hovered, looking around. Far below and behind him he could just make out Jabba's palace.

A steady stream of tiny bright objects flowed from it into the surrounding desert: speeders and sailbarges, doing Jabba's bidding.

A speeder could get me there in no time, Boba thought grimly. *No way I could steal one now, without getting caught.*

But a sailbarge . . .

He thought of the sailbarge that had brought him here. It had been crowded and disorderly, even with Jabba aboard.

But Jabba was in the palace now, along with Bib Fortuna. No one would be checking the barges as carefully as they had before.

Quickly Boba swooped down. He adjusted the jet pack's speed to save fuel. He'd need it later, when he got closer to Mos Espa. He flew as close to the gate as he could, squinting.

There!

A cargo skiff was angling its way out the gate. Its massive upper deck was covered with crates and empty cages. Boba could just make out a few droids on board, doing last-minute checks of the vessel's cargo. If he could just stay out of sight . . .

He brought himself down, silently, approaching the skiff from the side. Within the darkness of the open gate stood a few security guards. They were talking and laughing; they weren't doing their job.

Good thing! thought Boba. He steered the jet pack until he hung in the air just a few meters from the deck. Huge stacks of crates were there, secured with netting. There was a gap between one stack and the next. Too small for a human or Gamorrean guard, but just big enough — barely — for Boba. He looked around, making sure the guards were still distracted.

They were. Boba took a deep breath. He powered down on the jet pack until he was directly above the deck. He switched the power off and touched down, then darted between the stacks, his heart pounding.

Safe!

For now.

The skiff traveled for hours. Boba could see little, crouched where he was, so he used the time to rest. After a while, the rocking of the skiff lulled him to sleep. When finally he woke, Tatooine's two suns had traveled across the sky: It was late.

Wonder where we are? thought Boba. He peered out, but saw only endless dunes. Above him the sky shimmered with heat. He ducked back into his refuge, and once more tapped into his helmet's nav program.

"I need the coordinates for Mos Espa," he whispered. "Hope it's not far. . . ."

It wasn't. He checked his fuel levels: just enough to get him there. He stuck his head out and looked around.

There was no sign of security droids, or anyone else.

Boba's heart leaped with excitement. *Now or never!*

Then he leaped, too — up, up, up! The jet pack sent him arrowing into the sky. Below him the skiff shrank to almost nothing, a speck in an ocean of sand. Far, far behind him was Jabba's palace. Somewhere in front of him Mos Espa — and Boba's future — waited.

Boba soared on.

Below him the Dune Sea flashed past. He saw moisture farms, the metal carcass of an immense sand-wrecked freighter. He saw tiny outposts where the moisture farmers bought their supplies and traded water for food.

Once he saw the ground hundreds of meters below him shift and shudder like jelly. A Sarlaac was hunting beneath the sand.

He also saw a tiny black jot against the sky. It was many kilometers behind him.

But it was gaining.

It was Durge. Hunting Boba.

"Let's see if we can lose him," Boba said. Ahead he saw a long, ragged line in the sand.

A canyon.

He steered the jet pack so that he dropped into the canyon. It was ten or twenty kilometers long. And it was cooler than the open air high above.

Boba flew through it. He zigzagged along the canyon passage. He lifted his helmet and let the cool air touch his cheeks.

Then he saw the end of the canyon approaching. He lifted up, up into the hot dry air. He looked behind him.

There was no sign of Durge.

Lost him.

He looked ahead.

Ulp!

There, very close now, was Mos Espa.

And there, hovering just meters away from Boba, was Durge's speeder!

"Got you!" shouted Durge. He started to stand, a flamethrower at the ready. He took aim. The speeder rocked slightly as he got his balance.

"We'll see about that," retorted Boba. Stealthily he reached down for the ignition switch on his jet pack. He stared boldly at the armored bounty hunter.

"Three," counted Boba to himself. He watched Durge take aim. He waited until the very last second. "Two . . . one —"

Fire exploded from the flamethrower. At the same instant, the jet pack's flames went out. Boba dropped like a stone.

Where his head had been, a ball of fire burst.

Boba switched the jet pack back to full power. He somersaulted, kicking at the air until he was parallel to the ground far below. With a roar his jet pack sent him arrowing forward, beneath Durge's speeder.

"You —!"

Durge howled in rage. Another flamethrower burst exploded harmlessly behind Boba, then another. The speeder rocked as the bounty hunter jumped back behind his console. The vehicle turned to pursue Boba.

"I can outrun him," Boba said aloud. He wasn't sure if this was true. But he felt better saying it. "I can do this. . . ."

He looked up. Tatooine's two suns glared through the haze. Boba angled himself so that the suns were directly in front of him. If he did this right, their blaze might momentarily blind Durge.

And a moment was all Boba needed to escape!

He headed to where the bazaar was most crowded, vendors shouting their wares and hundreds of beings haggling for bargains.

"If I can get in there, I can lose him," said Boba. "Then I can find Ygabba . . ."

He glanced back. Sure enough, Durge's speeder had slowed. Boba could see the reflected glare of sunlight on Durge's body armor.

Boba looked ahead. There was no way Durge's speeder could manuever through the slow throng of shoppers.

"This is it," murmured Boba.

He cut back on his jet pack's power. His stomach seemed to drop from him as he fell forty meters. Almost immediately he powered back up and zoomed straight ahead. He raced just over the heads of the bewildered beings. He looked back.

Durge was out of sight. Boba had lost him!

He turned gleefully. He amped the jet pack's power to full.

Ahead of him was where he'd find Gilramos Libkath.

Ahead of him was triumph — or death.

CHAPTER TWENTY-THREE

Boba knew he would be easier to spot if he was flying.

"I should get down there," he said, staring at the maze of streets and alleys below. "I can hide from Durge, at least for a little while."

But he didn't have a little while. He had hardly any time at all.

And he didn't know exactly where Gilramos Libkath's lair was.

Boba frowned. He cruised slowly above cantinas and docking areas. In the distance, he saw the battered outline of Mentis Qinx's facility. He imagined he could see *Slave I*, waiting.

"I'll be there soon," he said.

He looked out again. Not very far off, a huge building rose. It nearly blotted out the sky.

The arena.

Gilramos's lair was near the arena!

He swerved, dropping until he flew only a few meters above the ground. A few merchants glared at him as they scurried past. Boba shrugged.

"Beats walking!" he yelled at them.

Ahead of him the main road ended abruptly. Boba surged upward, flying above a high wall. Beyond were more alleys. He saw water vendors arguing and a bantha waiting patiently outside a cantina door.

But he didn't see where Ygabba had taken him before.

He powered up, soaring a few meters higher. He looked down.

And saw it.

Below him was the familiar outline of a gutted Theed cruiser. Dead vegetation clung to its sides. Broken glass, scrap metal, and litter covered it.

To the casual viewer, it was just another wrecked starship.

To Boba, it was the first step toward freedom. *Here goes nothing.*

He powered down, trying to slow his descent. Still, when he touched down it was with a jolt.

"*Oooof!*"

He reached for the wall, steadying himself. He switched off his jet pack. He patted it.

"You sure came in handy," he said. "Remind me that I owe Gab'borah for this."

He lifted his helmet and wiped the sweat from his face. He was filthy, hot, and tired.

He was also very, very happy. He glanced up and down the alley to make sure no one saw him. He looked up.

No sign of Durge.

For now.

He turned. There was the doorway where he'd chased Ygabba. He took a deep breath. Then he pushed it open and went inside.

Darkness covered him like a cloak. Darkness, and cool air. Boba tapped his helmet, activating his infrared vision. Immediately, he could see.

Before him was a long tunnel. Eerie scarlet light glowed between the blackest shadows he had ever seen. He walked forward carefully. The floor was strewn with broken rubble. Bricks, empty water containers, remnants of food. Boba stopped and nudged something with his foot. He stooped to pick it up.

It was a label. The image of a fat Huttese face leered above a slogan.

GORGAL SPRINGS GENUINE PURE WATER
BESTINE'S FINEST

Ygabba had said the weapons shipment was hidden. It was inside a shipment from a moisture farm near Bestine.

It seemed ages ago, but he had only met Ygabba late yesterday. That was when she and the others had stolen the weapons. They would barely have had time to bring them here.

There would have been no time yet for Gilramos to claim his stolen goods.

He's here, Boba thought. *Right now — I can sense him.*

His neck prickled with fear. He began to walk very slowly through the red-lit room. When he reached the tunnel entrance he stopped.

He listened.

He could hear voices. One voice was anxious and pleading. The other was low and sly. It was a voice Boba would know anywhere. It was a voice he wouldn't trust for a nanosecond.

It was Gilramos Libkath.

CHAPTER TWENTY-FOUR

As silent as a breath, Boba entered the passage. As he walked the voices grew louder, until he could understand them.

"Master, we grabbed all we could. Then the guards saw him. I had no choice but to stop."

That voice was Ygabba's. She sounded desperate . . . and afraid.

"That is not good enough," someone hissed. Gilramos — the Neimoidian the children called Master. "There are very important people waiting for these illegal weapons — they aren't sold anywhere but the black market, and the buyers are relying on *me* to fill the order. You know what happens when you fail."

There was a sharp cry. Not Ygabba's voice.

It was the little boy, Murzz.

"Please don't hurt me!" he whimpered.

Boba's stomach tightened. Ahead of him a

bright patch blazed — the entrance to the central chamber. He switched off his infrared vision so he could see better. He crept forward.

"You know the agreement we made," Gilramos went on in his smooth, sickly voice.

Boba reached the opening. He crouched safely in the shadows. He stared inside.

In the center of the room stood the tall Neimoidian. His elaborate robes glowed purple and deep blue. His reptilian face was split by a sneer. At his feet sprawled a small figure — Murzz. Ygabba stood protectively beside him.

"Please, Master," she begged.

Boba shaded his eyes, squinting.

Was this another virtual image of Gilramos Libkath? Or was it really him?

The Neimoidian leaned forward. He grasped Murzz's shoulder. The boy cried out in fear and pain.

Boba's fists clenched angrily.

It was truly Gilramos, all right.

The Neimoidian's clawed hand tightened. His other hand gestured angrily.

"You have failed me! There are supposed to be seventeen cartons of weapons here! And how many do I see? Sixteen!"

Boba leaned forward to get a better look. Many crates were stacked around the perimeter of the room. Each had the same bright label.

GORGAL SPRINGS GENUINE PURE WATER

But some of the crates were open. And they did not contain water.

They were filled with weapons. Small missiles made with technology banned by the Republic.

Enough to outfit an army. And not an army of children, either. From the corner of his eye, Boba saw several battle droids, their armor gleaming in the shadows.

Boba jumped as Gilramos's voice rang out commandingly. "Who am I, children?" he demanded.

In the room around him, numerous small figures stood. Each raised a hand. In each hand an eye glowed.

"You are our Master, Libkath," the children said as one.

Gilramos nodded. "That is so. Who cares for you, children?"

"You do, Master."

The eyes glowed brighter. In the darkness, the battle droids moved, raising their arms menacingly.

Some of the children whimpered. Murzz kicked angrily at Gilramos.

"Let me go!" he shouted.

Gilramos only clutched him tighter.

"Who gives you refuge?" he said.

"You do, Master," repeated the children.

"That is so." The reptilian sneer became a scowl. Gilramos reached for Ygabba, grabbing her by the shoulder. "And what do I ask in return?"

"Obedience, Master."

"And if I do not receive it?"

Quickly Boba looked around. A pile of bricks stood near the entrance. He grabbed one.

"Answer me!" shouted Gilramos. He shook Ygabba angrily. "*If I do not receive obedience?*"

Boba crept to the very edge of the doorway. He took aim. He threw.

Bull's-eye!

With a grunt Gilramos staggered backward. His tall hat tottered then fell. He clutched his head. Immediately Ygabba grabbed Murzz and darted away. All around the room, children raised their hands. Shining eyes glowed brightly, then flickered. With an ominous whir, the battle droids moved into position.

"Who dares to strike me?" shouted Gilramos.

"Why don't you pick on someone closer to your own size?" Boba shouted back. He grabbed another brick and heaved it.

Bam!

This time Gilramos stumbled and nearly fell. With excited squeals the children raced away from him. They clambered up the walls, taking shelter on the shelves circling the room. Only Ygabba remained where she was, staring as Boba stepped into the room.

"Boba Fett!" she yelled. She grinned so broadly that for an instant he forgot about Gilramos and the droids.

"That's me!" Boba yelled back.

"Fett?" repeated Gilramos. He lurched up again. A trickle of pale yellow fluid ran down his face. "You dare to strike me?"

"That's right!" retorted Boba. He held up his hands, palm out. "You don't control me!"

"But I will!"

Gilramos raised his arm. A bolt of crimson light flowed from it. Was it some sort of power or just a trick? Boba wasn't about to find out. He ducked, then jammed on his jet pack. He soared upward, kicking at the Neimoidian's head.

"Argh!" shouted Gilramos. The battle droids froze, awaiting orders.

If I can just grab one of those weapons, I can blast him, and the droids! Boba thought. He angled toward an open crate. *Then I can claim Jabba's reward!*

The crate was just below him. Boba stretched his arm toward it. His fingers grazed a blaster's grip.

Wham!

Violet light jabbed at Boba's eyes. He cried out, then jolted upward. With a thud his head smashed into something.

The ceiling!

With a cry he fell.

CHAPTER TWENTY-FIVE

For a second all went black. Then Boba blinked and looked up. Above him a lizard face leered beneath an ornate mitred hat.

"Now what have we here?" Gilramos asked. He licked his thin lips. "A strong and clever boy. One who would make a fine addition to my army. After some modifications, of course."

He grabbed Boba's hand. Boba lashed out at him, but the Neimoidian was surprisingly strong.

"This will only take a moment," Gilramos said. Behind him the droids moved into formation, their weapons aimed at Boba. "And then . . ."

"The Mandalorian is mine!" thundered a voice.

Gilramos whirled. So did Boba.

"Durge," he whispered.

The bounty hunter's armored figure filled the entire doorway. In each massive arm he cradled a blaster. One was aimed at Gilramos's head. The other was aimed at Boba.

"One move and you'll be blasted into the Dune Sea!" Durge gloated.

Boba kicked at Gilramos. Durge took aim.

"Do you doubt me, runt?" Durge's eyes blazed.

He stepped into the room. Boba heard the hiss of the children breathing in sharply. The battle droids swiveled, their weapons pointing from Boba to Durge. Durge lifted his head. He looked around.

He smiled. A wide, horrible smile.

"So this is your army, eh, Gilramos?" He looked dismissively at the droids, then walked over and nudged a small girl with his blaster. "Thieving children and a handful of droids?"

Boba watched him. *If I only had a weapon,* he thought. *I could free us all!*

But could he? He glanced past where Gilramos held tightly to him.

There were crates of weaponry everywhere. One stray blast, and the whole place would become a weapon!

Wait a minute, Boba thought. From the corner of his eye he saw someone move. Not a droid. Not Gilramos, either.

Ygabba. She stood near a pile of crates. Her head turned. She looked desperately at Boba.

Immediately he knew what to do.

"Ygabba!" he shouted. "Lead them out! Run —
NOW!"

At the same time that Boba yelled, he flattened
himself against the floor. With a roar, Durge turned.
There was a flare of light from his blaster. Boba
kicked at Gilramos. The Neimoidian shrieked, then
tried to grab him. The droids surged forward.

Too late! Boba was free!

He slammed himself to the floor. Above him
Durge's blast struck Gilramos. The Neimoidian
fell. Another blast struck a droid with a muted explosion as the others tried to blast Durge.

"This way!" Ygabba shouted. "Fast!"

Like a flock of birds, the children scattered.
Ygabba stood by an opening and yelled at them.
Children raced everywhere. They dove through
holes in the walls. They clambered through gaps in
the ceiling. Everywhere glowing eyes shimmered
and shone as the children yanked one another to
safety.

All but Boba.

"Now you!" Durge roared. Another blast roared
from his weapon as a droid strode toward him. The
droid fell, and Durge laughed. "You're next!" he
cried, and aimed at Boba.

Boba glanced back. He saw Gilramos crawling
across the floor. His hat was beside him.

Neimoidians place huge value on their hats. Boba knew that. They represent power and prestige. No Neimoidian would ever be without one.

Not unless he was dead.

Boba grabbed the hat. Gilramos gave a desperate cry. *"No!"*

Boba turned. Another voice rose from the room. "Boba!"

He looked up. All of the children were gone — except for Ygabba. She stood by the open passage, waving at him. Beside her rose a pile of weapons.

"This way!" she shouted.

Boba clutched Gilramos's hat to him. He looked down at Durge, surrounded by the remaining battle droids. Boba reached for the ignition of his jet pack. He jammed it as hard as he could.

He flew.

"You die!" bellowed Durge. He swung around, the droids forgotten. His blasters pointed at Boba. Boba soared above him. He swooped down, one arm reaching for Ygabba.

"Grab hold!" Boba shouted.

She grabbed his hand. In front of him was the passage leading from the chamber. Behind him were Durge and the Neimoidian's droids.

"Hold tight!" Boba yelled.

He flew toward the pile of weapons. At the last

possible instant, he swerved, zooming into the tunnel.

"My hat!" screeched Gilramos. "Droids! Stop him!"

"Take that!" thundered Durge. And fired. This time his blast ricocheted into one of the crates.

Immediately the world exploded. Ygabba cried out, but she hung on. Boba kept his head down, soaring toward freedom. Behind them deafening explosions rocked the gutted Theed Cruiser.

"You okay?" shouted Boba above the din.

"You bet!" yelled Ygabba.

"Good! 'Cause we're almost out of here!"

Ahead of them, light bloomed. Behind them the explosions grew muted, like far-off thunder.

Moments later, they were outside again.

They were free.

CHAPTER TWENTY-SIX

"That was some entrance you made back there!" said Ygabba.

Boba nodded. He reached for the jet pack's ignition. They touched down.

"Yeah," he said, grinning. "And some exit, too!"

They ran until they were a safe distance from the alley.

"Don't worry," said Ygabba. She looked back. "Those Theed ships are built to withstand hyperspace. Everything inside may be gone. But the damage will be contained."

Boba nodded. A few meters away, a throng of small figures stood, watching them.

"Ygabba!" someone cried. "You made it!"

Ygabba ran up to them, beaming. The youngest children ran over to hug her. "I sure did — with a little help from my friend!"

She looked at Boba. He pushed back his helmet,

then glanced at what he still held — Gilramos's hat. He looked back and frowned.

"I don't know if he's gone or not," he said.

Ygabba walked over to him. She also looked back. "You're right," she said. "I don't think anyone could survive that, but . . ."

"Ygabba, look!"

Ygabba and Boba both turned.

Around them a circle of children raised their hands, palm out. Scores of glowing eyes stared at Boba, unblinking.

Then, like water seeping into dry sand, the eyes faded beneath their skin.

"They're gone!" gasped Murzz.

"Yes!" Boba punched his fist at the air triumphantly.

He raised Gilramos's hat above him. The children cheered.

"What about Durge?" said Ygabba.

Boba's face clouded.

"Good question," he said. He looked at the alley. Smoke crept along the ground. "He might be dead. But I wouldn't bet on it."

Thoughtfully, Boba fingered the ignition of his jet pack. He glanced at the fuel tanks.

"They're nearly empty," he said. He pushed his helmet farther back on his head. He stared at

Ygabba. "Now what? How can I return to Jabba's fortress? I can't afford to pay for the repairs on my starship until Jabba pays *me.*"

Ygabba looked at him. She grinned. "Wait one minute," she said.

She turned and called the children to her. "All of you, listen. You know where Bley-san's cantina is?"

The children nodded. "Great," said Ygabba. She smiled at them encouragingly, then stooped. "I want all of you to go there. Ask for Bley-san. She owes me a favor. Tell her I sent you. She will help you find your parents or relatives. She will help you get home."

Ygabba straightened. "Bley-san is a good woman," she said. "You can trust her. Now go! Remember, you're free now!"

Laughing in delight, the children swarmed around Ygabba. They hugged her and called out their good-byes.

"Wait a minute," said Ygabba. She held up a hand and turned. She looked at Boba. Then she looked at the children. She asked, "Aren't you all forgetting something?"

The children turned. They looked at Boba. They raised their hands — empty palms now, except for dirt and soot. They smiled.

"Thank you, Boba Fett!" they shouted. Then, giggling, they turned and ran to find Bley-san's cantina.

Boba watched them go. He felt something he had never felt before.

Happiness. But also pride.

"Well," he said when the children were out of sight. "We'd better leave, too."

Ygabba cocked a thumb at him.

"Come here," she said. She began to hurry down the alley.

Boba followed her. As they rounded a curve, she stopped.

"Check it out," she said.

In front of them hovered a sleek cruiser.

"Wow," breathed Boba. "That's beautiful! Who's is it?"

"Mine," said Ygabba. At Boba's surprised look, she shrugged. "Well, it was Master Libkath's. But I figure he owes it to me."

Boba didn't argue. He watched as Ygabba walked over and punched an access code into a panel. Immediately, the top popped open. Ygabba swung herself inside. She motioned for Boba to join her. The cover snapped shut. The cruiser began to rise. Boba lowered his helmet. He put Gilramos's hat on his lap.

"Do you know how to fly this thing?" asked Ygabba.

Boba smiled. He took the controls. The cruiser leaped through the air

"Next stop, Jabba's fortress!" he cried.

CHAPTER TWENTY-SEVEN

It was night when they finally arrived at the palace of Jabba the Hutt. They docked the cruiser, then headed for the main gate.

Armed sentries guarded the huge iron door. But when Boba displayed Gilramos's hat, they looked impressed.

"You may pass," a sentry said. He looked at Boba, then cocked his thumb. "But not her."

"She's with me," snapped Boba. "Or do you want to discuss this matter with Jabba?"

The guard grumbled. But he let them go.

"They seem to know you," said Ygabba. She looked at Boba admiringly.

"Yeah, I get around," he said.

They approached Jabba's throne room. Noises of merriment greeted them.

"Sounds like a feast in progress," said Boba. They went inside.

To judge by the mess, the feast was nearly over.

Empty plates covered a long table. Guests reclined in chairs, or milled around, talking. On his throne sat Jabba. He greedily ate handfuls of worms. Now and then he would take a long drink from a bubbling tube. Then he belched noisily and laughed.

"Looks like we missed dinner," said Boba.

"No," said Ygabba. She pointed. "Look there."

At the end of the table closest to Jabba, there were still numerous plates. Each held a brightly colored cake. Several were topped by waving eyestalks. Boba glanced at them, then at Jabba.

"O Mightiest of Hutts!" he cried. He strode toward the throne. "I have done as you wished."

Jabba stared down at him as though he were another wriggling worm. Then he saw the ornate hat that Boba held toward him.

"Give me that," rumbled Jabba.

Boba handed him the hat. Jabba took it. He held it up to the light. He examined it thoroughly. He sniffed it.

"It stinks of treachery!" he boomed. "It stinks of Gilramos Libkath!"

Beside Jabba, Bib Fortuna whispered, "But can we be sure he is dead?"

Jabba looked at him disdainfully. "No Neimoidian would ever part with his hat!"

He leaned over and dropped it into a smoking

pot. Immediately, flames leaped up. In moments, the hat was gone. Only ash remained.

"You have done well!" Jabba cried. Then his eyes narrowed. "But what of Durge?"

Boba shook his head. "Do you see him here, O Great Jabba?" he asked loudly. "He has failed. And I — I have triumphed!"

Jabba looked at him. He nodded. He raised his arms to his guests. "All of you, listen! This young warrior has succeeded where others have failed! Great rewards shall come to you, you —" He stared down at Boba. "What is your name, Mandalorian?"

"Boba. Boba Fett."

"Boba Fett!" repeated Jabba.

In the room around Boba, everyone applauded.

"Way to go!" said Ygabba. She gave his arm a friendly punch.

"Thank you, O Jabba," said Boba. He bowed. *Better not forget that!* he thought.

"Arrange for his bounty," Jabba commanded Bib Fortuna.

The Twi'lek major-domo nodded. He stepped down from the throne platform and walked to Boba. He handed him a gleaming chip.

"Your pay," he said.

Boba took the chip. He removed his helmet and

slung it over his arm. As he stared at the chip his eyes grew wide.

This is enough to outfit Slave I *three times over!* he thought.

"I have other jobs for you — many of them!" rumbled Jabba the Hutt.

Boba nodded. He took a step backward, Ygabba beside him.

"You think we can eat now?" she whispered.

"I sure hope so," he whispered back.

He looked up once more at Jabba the Hutt. But the gang lord's attention had already turned to other matters.

"Quick," said Ygabba, yanking Boba toward the table. "Before he gives you something else to do!"

But as they approached the table, Ygabba's expression grew sad. Boba looked at her, then at the many plates. They all held desserts — cakes, puddings, viral jellies, wuorl-pies.

"Aren't you hungry?" he began. "I thought you said —"

Suddenly Ygabba's face went pale. She stared in front of her. She gasped.

"Father!" she cried.

Boba turned. At the end of the table a frail figure stood. He wore a bright green cook's robes and hat. In his hand was a jeweled Vortexian cake knife. As he stared at Ygabba, he too went white.

He exclaimed, "Daughter!"

Boba watched as the two embraced. Ygabba was crying. So was Gab'borah.

"How can this be?" the old man asked. He looked past her, to where Boba stood. "You —?"

Ygabba nodded. "It was him, Father. He saved us, all of us. From Gilramos Libkath."

"Libkath," murmured Gab'borah. He looked as though he were dreaming. "Five years ago, he kidnapped her. That was before Jabba brought me here, as his chef. . . ."

He reached a thin hand to Boba. "Young man, I owe you my heart," he said. "And my daughter's life. Thank you."

Boba shrugged. Then he smiled. "You're welcome."

Gab'borah waved him closer. "Come here!" he said.

He pointed at a cake. It was as tall as Boba, and topped with scry-mint frosting and vannilan pods. At its peak was a Ziziibbon truffle that shone like a gem.

Boba set his helmet on the floor. He slid his credit chip into his pocket, safe beside his father's book. Behind him a voice boomed.

"Do not get too distracted, young man!" Jabba pointed at him. "Tomorrow morning you begin your new life!"

Boba nodded. He thought of *Slave I* waiting for him back in the spaceport. Then he watched as Gab'borah plucked the luscious truffle from the cake and handed it to him.

"Eat!" Gab'borah commanded.

Boba took the candy, grinning.

"Thanks," he said.

At last! An order he was happy to obey!

He heard Jabba laugh and knew — he'd found his future at last.

CLONE WARS
TIMELINE

With the Battle of Geonosis (Episode II), the Republic is plunged into an emerging, galaxy-wide conflict. On one side, the Confederacy of Independent Systems (the Separatists), led by the charismatic Count Dooku and backed by a number of powerful guilds and trade organizations, and their droid armies.

On the other side, the Republic loyalists and their newly created clone army, led by the Jedi. It is a war fought on a thousand fronts, with heroism and sacrifices on both sides. Below is a partial list of some of the important events of the Clone Wars and a guide to where these events are chronicled.

MONTHS (after *Attack of the Clones*)	EVENT

0   **THE BATTLE OF GEONOSIS**
Star Wars: Episode II *Attack of the Clones* (LFL, May '02)

0   **THE SEARCH FOR COUNT DOOKU**
Boba Fett #1: *The Fight to Survive* (SB, April '02)

+1   **THE BATTLE OF RAXUS PRIME**
Boba Fett #2: *Crossfire* (SB, November '02)

+1   **THE DARK REAPER PROJECT**
The Clone Wars (LEC, May '02)

+1.5   **CONSPIRACY ON AARGAU**
Boba Fett #3: *Maze of Deception* (SB, April '03)

+2   **THE BATTLE OF KAMINO**
Clone Wars I: *The Defense of Kamino* (DH, June '03)

+2   **DURGE VS. BOBA FETT**
Boba Fett #4: *Hunted* (SB, October '03)

+2.5   **THE DEFENSE OF NABOO**
Clone Wars II: *Heroes and Scapegoats* (DH, September '03)

+6   **THE HARUUN KAL CRISIS**
Mace Windu: *Shatterpoint* (DR, June '03)

+9   **THE DAGU REVOLT**
Escape from Dagu (DR, March '04)

+12   **THE BIO-DROID THREAT**
The Cestus Deception (DR, June '04)

+15   **THE BATTLE OF JABIIM**
Clone Wars III: *Last Stand on Jabiim* (DH, February '04)

+24   **THE CASULTIES OF DRONGAR**
MedStar Duology: *Battle Surgeons* (DR, July '04)
          Healer (DR, October '04)

+30   **THE PRAESITLYN CONQUEST**
Jedi Trail (DR, November '04)

KEY:

DH = *Dark Horse Comics, graphic novels* www.darkhorse.com

DR = *Del Rey, hardcover & paperback books* www.delreydigital.com

LEC = *LucasArts Games, games for XBox, Game Cube, PS2, & PC platforms* www.lucasarts.com

LFL = *Lucasfilm Ltd., motion pictures* www.starwars.com

SB = *Scholastic Books, juvenile fiction* www.scholastic.com/starwars

STAR WARS

JEDI QUEST

___	0-439-33917-0	STAR WARS: JEDI QUEST #01: THE WAY OF THE APPRENTICE	$4.99
___	0-439-33918-9	STAR WARS: JEDI QUEST #02: THE TRAIL OF THE JEDI	$4.99
___	0-439-33919-7	STAR WARS: JEDI QUEST #03: THE DANGEROUS GAMES	$4.99
___	0-439-33920-0	STAR WARS: JEDI QUEST #04: THE MASTER OF DISGUISE	$4.99
___	0-439-33921-9	STAR WARS: JEDI QUEST #05: THE SCHOOL OF FEAR	$4.99
___	0-439-33922-7	STAR WARS: JEDI QUEST #06: THE SHADOW TRAP	$4.99
___	0-439-33923-5	STAR WARS: JEDI QUEST #07: THE MOMENT OF TRUTH	$4.99
___	0-439-24204-5	STAR WARS: JEDI QUEST: THE PATH TO TRUTH (Hardcover)	$12.95

Available wherever you buy books, or use this order form.

Scholastic Inc., P.O. Box 7502, Jefferson City, MO 65102

Please send me the books I have checked above. I am enclosing $_____ (please add $2.00 to cover shipping and handling). Send check or money order — no cash or C.O.D.s please.

Name_____ Birth date_____

Address_____

City_____ State/Zip_____

Please allow four to six weeks for delivery. Offer good in U.S.A. only. Sorry, mail orders are not available to residents of Canada. Prices subject to change.

www.scholastic.com/starwars

SCHOLASTIC

SWJQBL1003